Sarah A. Dorsey

Panola

a tale of Louisiana

Sarah A. Dorsey

Panola
a tale of Louisiana

ISBN/EAN: 9783337343996

Printed in Europe, USA, Canada, Australia, Japan

Cover: Foto ©Andreas Hilbeck / pixelio.de

More available books at **www.hansebooks.com**

PANOLA.

A TALE OF LOUISIANA.

BY MRS. SARAH A. DORSEY.

AUTHOR OF

"AGNES GRAHAM," "ATHALIE," "LUCIA DARE."

"A seaside house to the farther South,
Where the baked cicalas die of drouth,
And one sharp tree—'tis a cypress—stands
By the many hundred years red-rusted,
Rough, iron-spiked, ripe fruit o'er-crusted—
My sentinel to guard the sands
To the water's edge.
  *   *   *   *   *
While in the house forever crumbles
Some fragment of the frescoed walls
From blisters where a scorpion sprawls—
A girl bare-footed brings, and tumbles
Down on the pavement, green flesh melons."

PHILADELPHIA:

T. B. PETERSON & BROTHERS;

306 CHESTNUT STREET.

MRS. SARAH A. DORSEY'S WORKS.

Each Work is complete in one large Volume.

PANOLA. *A Tale of Louisiana.* By MRS. SARAH A. DORSEY. One volume, duodecimo, cloth, black and gold, price $1.50.

Read the following notice of "Panola," written by Dr. Mackenzie, Literary Editor of Forney's Daily Press, who read the work in manuscript.

"PANOLA," a Tale of Louisiana, is from the pen of Mrs. Sarah A. Dorsey, a talented and highly educated lady, distinguished in biography and romance. The story is very peculiar, and strikingly original, in its philosophy, its individuality of characters, and the successive steps in the narrative by which the action culminates in a very striking and most unexpected, though highly satisfactory conclusion. Life in the south-western part of Louisiana is represented with a brilliancy of description which, indeed, is word-painting of the most artistical order. The dialogue really advances the action, (which dialogue too often fails to do,) and in the few letters that are introduced, the *dramatis personæ* respectively give their views of society. Although Panola, a bright and lovely child of genius, who is a natural musician, is the principal heroine—a veritable *prima donna* in more ways than one—there is a rival, scarcely less beautiful if somewhat less excellent. There are two lovers, to maintain the balance—but the best of these has unfortunately lost the use of his limbs—like the young King of the Black Islands, of the Arabian tale, who was half man and half marble. Under such circumstances, this gentleman would scarcely have his name written, by a fashionable mother, on the list of "eligible" candidates for her fair daughter's hand! Nevertheless, he does contrive to marry the "ladye of his love," to the perfect satisfaction of both, though the preliminary miracle which enabled this to be done is to be found only in the closing chapters of the story. Panola has Cherokee blood in her veins, and some of her race prove, in this story, that they indeed are "Children of the Sun with whom Revenge is virtue." The book abounds in interest—marriage, divorce, a great musician's *debut* and triumph, the alternations of various and conflicting passions—death by poison, and the already hinted punishment of the criminal. Two very interesting characters are an old French Doctor of medicine and a German naturalist. As the "universal dollar" manages to work itself into everything below, we may hint that a trifle of over three millions is a bequest in the very first chapter.

AGNES GRAHAM. *A Novel.* By MRS. SARAH A. DORSEY. One volume, octavo, paper cover, price Sixty Cents.

ATHALIE. *"A Winter's Tale."* By MRS. SARAH A. DORSEY. One volume, octavo, paper cover, price Sixty Cents.

LUCIA DARE. *A Novel.* By MRS. SARAH A. DORSEY. One volume, octavo, paper cover, price Sixty Cents.

TO A MAN WHOSE RARE FIDELITY IN FRIENDSHIP IS A THEME
OF ADMIRATION FOR ALL WHO KNOW HIM.

TO

COLONEL JOHN M. SANDIDGE,

OF LOUISIANA,

THIS BOOK IS INSCRIBED BY ONE WHO IS GLAD TO WRITE
HERSELF AMONG THE NUMBER OF HIS FRIENDS.

Elkridge, Tensas Parish,
August 20th, 1877.

—

CONTENTS.

(21)

"A seaside house to the farther South,
  Where the baked cicalas die of drouth,
    And one sharp tree—'tis a cypress—stands
By the many hundred years red-rusted,
Rough, iron-spiked, ripe fruit o'er-crusted—
    My sentinel to guard the sands
      To the water's edge.

*　　*　　*　　*　　*　　*

While in the house forever crumbles
  Some fragment of the frescoed walls
  From blisters where a scorpion sprawls—
A girl bare-footed brings, and tumbles
  Down on the pavement, green flesh melons."

BROWNING.

"We are the sum of our ancestors—plus—ourselves."

ANNE SEEMULLER.

PANOLA.

CHAPTER I.

IN THE ATTAKAPAS.

THE day was beautiful. The sunshine of May poured all over and, it seemed, all through the very earth, in the country of "The Attakapas." The yellow jasmine flung its garlands of golden, perfumed chalices around the very tops of the tallest forest trees, mingling its flowers with the streamers of venerable gray Spanish moss (Tillandsia), which draped the huge branches, and which waved with silvery, undulating gleams in the breezy sunshine. The Cherokee rose flaunted its long pennons of great white flowers and small, dark, glistering leaves over miles and miles of hedge rows. The red-bud (Judas tree) was set thickly in spikes of blooms, the white locust hung its cornucopiæ of honey-smelling papilionaceous blossoms high above the huge rose hedges, and its blossoms were filled with

(25)

myriads of busy humming bees.   As for butterflies,
who could number them ?

There were every sort of the day butterflies, who
have knobs at the end of their antennæ ; the asterias,
and the yellow philodice, and the beautiful deiopeiæ ;
the phœton and the vanessas ; the admiral, the this-
tle, and the golden C. vanessas ; the troilus, the
philenor, the Danaus, and the idalias—all the
aristocratic idlers, who, clothed with silver and gold
and purple, ornamented with ever-varying splendor,
have naught to do but to seek their own pleasure
and spend their life of a summer day in fluttering
from bough to bough, satiating themselves with
sweetest nectar.

The butterflies had a pretty good time of it if
they escaped the beaks of the mocking-birds, during
the caterpillar period ; it was rare that the birds
attacked the full-grown insect, though sometimes
one might see the very poetry of the chase in a
mocking-bird's pursuit after a fluttering yellow
colias, which it always caught and flew away with,
bearing it off with the golden wings quivering at
the end of its curved bill.   It was pretty to see,
though sad for the insect, of course.

The ground was carpeted on the wide prairies
with acres and acres of precious little Houstonias, the
"Child's Delight," as the Southern people call them,
more poetically than the wise botanists.   The mocking-birds were singing their very maddest bursts of

delirious music. Spring-life is strong in this semi-tropical land! Cardinal birds, in brilliant groups of carmine, pecking the bright green grass, occasionally stopped to sing their little song of "Sweetie, sweetie, sweetie." Blue-birds flitted about, like bits shed out of the azure sky. Whole flocks of lovely little swamp warblers, green and gold, red and yellow, blue and brown, of every tint and changeful sheen of color, would suddenly drop upon the emerald herbage (like a cloud of flakes from a broken rainbow), hop, twitter, then fly up and disappear in the sun-lighted air as quickly as they had come. Humming-birds beat their wings, vibrating from umbel to umbel of the scarlet Yecoma trumpets, and the lilac bunches of the China tree (Melia Azadarach) were the chosen haunts of the tiny mango colibri. Turtle-doves sang softly and mournfully their invitation to their mates, "Come into the woods! Come into the woods!" The fig trees were pushing young, green leaflets. Grape vines, in flower, pulsated puffs of incense on the warm air. Orange trees, in stately rows, were showering cream-white petals down upon the wide sheets of cotton cloth, that Lizbette had spread so carefully under their boughs in order to catch cast-off corollas; for Lizbette was a skilful compounder of all sorts of orange syrups and citron confections. Was she not a "cordon bleu," "nata" as well as "fit" among Creole cooks? Whose orange-flower

water was better and more soothing to weak nerves,
or better known than hers? Who understood as
she did the manufacture of the delicate *Pralines*
of the stewed orange-petals, after the syrup had been
perfected? Whose liqueur of the passion flowers
was clearer and stronger than hers? Surely for
these things Lizbette was widely famed throughout
the whole of the Attakapas.

It was Docteur Canonge's house. "Le Docteur
Renée Canonge." So the people called him in the
Attakapas. In France, when people spoke of him
—and people did speak of him there sometimes, in
the scientific academies and such-like places—he was
called "Monsieur lé Marquis de Canonge, et de
Rocheterre."

Lizbette never forgot this fact, if other people
did. Why should she? Was she not the chief
"*cuisinière*," the cook of the family, and in her own
opinion the chief governor of the whole establishment? And did she not reflect all its dignity?
Ah, bah! Lizbette snapped her fingers in the faces
of cooks of roturiers, and such-like vulgar persons.
She always wore a gay-colored bandana kerchief
tied high, like a helmet, with an outflying plaited
shell of starched ends over each ear. No one but
Lizbette could solve the mystery of the plaiting of
that handkerchief! It could only be fashioned by
a Louisiana quadroon!

Immediately about the house there was a trim

flower-garden enclosed by a thick hedge of the Laurier d'amande, cut into a square, low wall of verdure.
Inside of this garden there were grotesque chairs,
and flat tables, and umbrellas, and pyramids and
cubes and griffins cut out of the same plants, whose
glossy leaves are so readily clipped and trained into
any fantastic form. This parterre was somewhat
formal, but it was queer and pretty and so very
French, that it was pleasant to look at. It had
character.

L' esprit Gaulois was stamped on every line of it.
It had all the old-fashioned favorite French flowers
in its funny little beds; each bed was carefully
bordered with red bricks, and inside of the bricks
grew, around each bed, a row of double violets,
now all blossoming and very fragrant. There were
lots of mignonette, and of carnations, of clove pinks
and pansies; also bunches of fleur d' lis in the
corners. Lizbette used to make calamus of the
sweet flag-roots, and she used the violets and rose
leaves for tisane. She also used the lavender and
verbena grasses among her linen; and of the fennel
and grape leaves she used many to green her
pickles. Marigolds and sweet bay and rosemary
served for seasoning soups; and of the glorious lilies,
the candidum, which reverent painters put into the
Virgin's hands, Lizbette made a fine healing salve
for cuts and burns. So it was for that they grew,
Lizbette believed. What did she care for their

beauty? Lizbette was eminently practical in all her ideas!

The garden walks were cemented with yellow plaster, and there were numbers of very ugly earthenware vases filled with verbenas and gay petunias; and some curiously moulded and much dilapidated plaster statues were planted and scattered about in secluded nooks, as well as at intervals along the garden walks. They were originally intended to increase the general effect of " Watteau-happy-shepherdistic existence." They were now either fantastically ludicrous, or mournfully suggestive, as one happened to be in the humor of either laughing or moralizing. These mutilated statues and vases were all elevated on low pedestals of brick and mason work, off which the stucco had crumbled long ago, and it had never been renewed. So they presented rather a spotty appearance, except in the vases, where the luxuriance of the growing vines helped to conceal these ravages of time; for sometimes they overflowed the vases and clambered down their sides and along the pedestals down to the very earth, where they took root and flourished vigorously. Things do grow so fast in Louisiana. Docteur Canonge's old gardener could never keep up with them, no matter how industriously he labored. He had to rest a good deal in the course of the day; there were pipes to be smoked full of good perrique, and there was also a siesta to be taken every afternoon. Therefore vines and weeds did grow rather as they chose in this garden. It was all the nicer for that.

The house itself was shadowed by its long, wide verandahs. It was a low, one-storied building. It was painted outside of a brick-dust red—the red of Titian, which is prettier on the mantle of the "Bella donna" than it was on Docteur Canonge's house—and it had solid green blinds, hung with white facings to the numerous doors and windows cut down to the verandah floors. Fortunately the paint was old, so Nature, with her gradating fingers, had toned it down comfortably from its original brilliant hues, with fine black weather stains, and lovely spottings of good wholesome dark chocolate-brown earth color.

It looked very well now, amidst its vast setting of yellowish, green prairie, and dome of blue sky.

Amidst all the other birds, the mocking-birds reigned supremely over this garden. They fought and mocked all the other birds, and they ate the butterflies and the caterpillars, and pecked the fruit, especially the ripest figs and the sunniest side of the peaches. They devoured as many scuppernong grapes as they chose, and always ate up the earliest peas and strawberries. The gardener complained and Lizbette quarrelled, but Docteur Canonge said the mocking-birds were not to be touched or frightened by any one whilst they lived upon his premises.

"So," Lizbette said, with a shrug of her shoulders, "the foot of the docteur was put down in regard to those birds." It was more than Lizbette dared to do, to disturb a nest, even though an aggravating pair had built in the orange tree over her own chamber window, and often kept her awake half the moonlight nights, singing and imitating the very cries and cluckings even of her own chickens, and anything else they took a fancy to mock. Ah! it was indeed exasperating; but then, the docteur's foot was down, and it had to be borne with such patience as a Creole cook could gather together.

This very morning, Lizbette had seen Natika Jacquimin, the old docteur's granddaughter, now on a visit to him, leaning on the balustrade of the verandah for a whole half-hour, extremely amused in watching the birds' antics. It was a triumph to keep Natika interested so long a time as that; but the feathered songsters were unconscious of their glory; they were dancing together, turning somersaults in the air, singing away like little possessed demons, unmindful of the beautiful girl who was patiently watching their pranks.

"Chee-chee," said Lizbette, "always a cheeing and a screeching, and a dancing like mad; and good for nuthin'; not even fit for a pie, which doves is, and even yellow-hammers ain't bad for a broil!"

Natika had been laughing heartily, and she called aloud to her two cousins, who were sitting quietly inside of the study, to look out at the birds. There was a young bird who seemed to be taking his first singing lessons. He had been attracted by the soft, sweet cry of a partridge, and he was trying to imitate it. He did not succeed well. An older bird, who was sitting on top of the head of a broken-nosed plaster Apollo, attempted to put the little bird right in the singing: the wilful little bird either couldn't or wouldn't follow the notes accurately. Another bird, balancing himself on an orange bough, quivering his wings and vibrating his tail fan-fashion, sending down at every trill a rain of spent blossoms upon Lizbette's sheets, was singing very heroically, loudly mocking the clear bell-like call of the troopiall; it had come across some stray wanderer from the tropics, blown over from some of the islands in the Gulf of Mexico, by an unexpected "ouragan," and, as is the fashion of its tribe, it had picked up the singular foreign notes.

The partridge sang "Bob white" in a long modulation; the little bird would snatch up the cry, "Bob, bob, bob; white, white, bob."

"No, no," the older bird sung from the Apollo's head; "this way: bob white, bob white."

"Why-et, why-et, bob, bob," would answer the small bird on the garden walk. Again and again the older bird would sing the strain.

The little bird, turning its head first on one side and then on the other, would listen carefully and

2

make ineffectual efforts to utter the right cadence; but at last, seeming to grow weary of its abortive efforts, and impatient of its lesson, it flew off on to a Laurier d'amande bush, and standing up on its tip-toes, with its wings outspread, and its head and tail tossed upwards, it sung vehemently after its own fashion: "Bob, bob; why-et, why-et; sweetie, sweetie, chee, chee; come to the wood; come, come, bob;" then, trilling on every syllable, it seemed to play on the notes with an appoggiatura before each word, as if to say, "how are ye, bob? how are ye, why-et?" then, suddenly seizing the easier strain, it closed its musical phrase with the three clear, pure bell-notes of the troopiall. It had its own notion of rendering music. Natika laughed and clapped her hands lightly. "Bravo! bravo! you naughty, funny little bird!" she cried.

Her cousins, Victor Burthe and Mark Bolling, smiled at her eagerness.

The cousins had been sitting together in the study, whose tall windows were widely opened down to the verandah. Natika stepped back into the room. Mark Bolling was reading a letter which a servant had just brought in to him, he said, by order of his grandfather, Docteur Canonge. Mark's face changed from its smile as he read the letter through carefully; then, turning it again, re-read the first page. He then handed it to Victor, saying, quietly:

"Uncle Jacob is dead in New York. This letter concerns you both, as well as myself."

It was a large letter, and it contained an enclosure written on foolscap, very closely covering all four sides of the sheet. Mark now set himself to read the enclosed foolscap.

Victor held the letter, and Natika, leaning over his shoulder, read it at the same time that he did. Victor gave utterance to a low whistle of surprise and seeming vexation as he laid the letter down, which ran as follows:

"NEW ORLEANS, 18—.

"Mr. MARK BOLLING : SIR :—We have been requested by the trustees appointed in the last will and testament of your late uncle, Mr. Jacob Canonge, to write to you, and to enclose a certified copy of said will and testament of said Jacob Canonge. Said will is a holograph instrument, and is perfect according to law of Louisiana, being written, signed and sealed by said testator. It has been duly recorded by said trustees, and the succession is now duly opened according to law. The said will is somewhat peculiar in its terms and conditions of bequest, which, of course, we regret ; but, although the said late Jacob Canonge was regarded as rather eccentric in character, his sound health and sanity were never questioned, and he was considered to be singularly shrewd in all practical business matters. His physicians—the Doc-

tors Stone and Roussel—testify to his admirable
soundness of mind up to the very last moments of
existence. The injunctions of the will, therefore,
must be fully obeyed. The trustees—Messrs.
Adams, James and Slocumb—unite with us in
hoping that you may soon be restored to the health
and happy condition of life, which said will demands of you before they can resign to you the control of the vast wealth, designed for your inheritance by your late uncle, said late Jacob Canonge.
Together with this, please find notices to the other
heirs—Mr. Victor Burthe and Miss Natika Jacquimin—of their unconditioned bequests from their
late uncle, said late Jacob Canonge, which bequests
are in the sum of one hundred thousand dollars
each, said money being now on deposit in the Canal
Bank of New Orleans, subject to their order at sight.
Please also find list and vouchers of said divers
moneys, bequeathed conditionally to you by said late
Jacob Canonge—said moneys amounting, as shown
and exhibited by said vouchers, to the sum of three
millions five hundred thousand and forty-five dollars and fifty-five cents, which is already well and
sufficiently invested by said late Jacob Canonge, as
shown by said vouchers. All to be subject to your
order under certain conditions, as set forth in said
last will and testament of said late Jacob Canonge.

"You will be so good as to notify us where and
when you desire to be deposited the annual pay-

ments of the sum of three hundred dollars, always payable in gold, the amount specified as a temporary provision for you until the aforesaid conditions be filled as demanded by said last will and testament of said late Jacob Canonge. It is now subject to your order.

"With profound respect, we have the honor to subscribe ourselves your most obedient servants,

"BRADFORD AND BRADFORD,

"Att'ys-at-Law, 20 Custom House street,

"New Orleans, Louisiana."

"Here's the will," said Mark, handing the long bit of foolscap he had been reading to Victor.

"It is a shame! The very meanest will that ever any old man made! That's my opinion of it," exclaimed Natika, indignantly, tossing back, with her fair, white, jewelled hand, the heavy ringlets that had fallen forward over her face as she leaned over Victor's shoulder reading the portentous papers.

"He was a mean, crabbed old hunks, any how! I always did think so," said Victor. "He has been too good to us, who did not need his dirty money. But, to treat poor Mark in that tantalizing fashion! It is downright wicked! I hope the old fellow will be put through three millions of ages in purgatory for his malice! As if it was Mark's fault that he can't walk! Oh, le vieil diable!"

"Le vieil Adam!" added Natika, laughing at Victor's violence.

"Oh, no!" said Mark, "un pauvre *vieux* homme. Not the man of sin or the old devil either."

"Yes! He *was* an old devil," said Natika, resolutely. "As for me, I intend to divide with you, Mark. I shall write instantly to those tiresome lawyers. I shall not remain a party to such meanness as that!" Here Natika violently stamped her small foot in its black satin slipper.

"I have plenty of money of my own without this, and so also has Victor. I never did like uncle Jacob. His nose was crooked, and his chin too, and he looked exactly like those misers in Quentin Matsys' picture. Don't you remember, Victor? And how I used to cry at the sight of him when I was *so* little, and he glowered at me through his old black-rimmed spectacles! I hate spectacles, and I hate misers. Mark is the only one of us that ever was decently respectful to uncle Jacob.

"Don't you remember how you sketched his profile on the wall one night with a bit of charcoal, when he came to see aunt Burthe, Victor? It was a very good likeness. Aunt Burthe scolded, but uncle Jacob laughed at it and said you ought to be made a painter of, and offered to pay for your instruction in art. We don't deserve one cent from uncle Jacob, and I sha'n't take it. Victor may do as he likes, but I shall not take the money. I *hate* uncle Jacob!" added she, passionately. "I am glad he is dead. He should not have been let to live so long. Just to die and make people so very unhappy as he has done now!"

"It is very good of you, Natika," said Mark Bolling, passing his hand wearily over his forehead and eyes, leaning back helplessly in his invalid's chair. "But it would be impossible for me to take such advantage of your generosity. I can't receive anything but the three hundred per annum that uncle Jacob has seen fit to give to me. Of course the rest of the estate will remain intact and accumulate during my unfortunate existence for '*the Charity.*' In all human probability I can never claim it. It is not probable; ah, it is scarcely even possible, that I shall ever be able '*to walk,*' still less that I should ever be so fortunate as '*to marry,*' as the will requires I should, before I can claim the millions uncle Jacob has left behind him. Indeed, the money would be of small value to me, if the qualities needed to possess it were ever mine. Oh, if I could ever hope to walk again! If I *could* ever dare to think of love as other men do! I should care but little for money. But to be so helpless, so dependent!"

Mark sighed deeply. "And alas! *so young,*" added he, with a smile of bitter sadness. "I shall have to live a long time yet, I fear."

Natika's eyes filled with large tears, as she looked

at Mark. He was so handsome, so attractive in person and character; and he sat there helpless as the prince of the black isles in the fairy tale. His lower limbs still perfect in outline, and yet utterly useless and apparently immovable. Mark was paralyzed from the waist downward; yet there was no appearance of wasting away in his figure. He was a picture of manly health and beauty as he sat still in his chair before her eyes.

"Confound it!" exclaimed Victor Burthe, springing up and kicking Natika's white poodle out of his way, as he strode up to Mark and seized his hand in both of his. "I say, Mark," continued Victor, unmindful of the yelping of the poodle, or of the angry exclamation of Natika at its treatment, or her ineffectual attempts to console her dog's injured feelings.

"I say, Mark! (For *heaven's* sake, Natika, do stop *that* wretched beast's mouth! Choke him.) I say, Mark, be reasonable now, and let us divide, Natika and I. Let us throw it all into three parts and each take one, and let the rest go to the d——d Charity, according to the will."

"Oh, no, Victor!" replied Mark, firmly, pressing Victor's hand. "It is utterly impossible. I *cannot;* believe I am not ungrateful, however, to you and to Natika," and Mark held out his other hand to Natika. She put down the poodle, whose cries had gradually subsided under her caresses, and took Mark's hand in hers. Mark drew her to him, and held up his mouth to kiss her.

Natika kissed him—her face flushed crimson as her lips met his, but she said nothing. Mark put his arm around her waist as she stood by him, and clasped Victor's hand yet more strongly.

"Dear cousins mine," said Mark, in a voice broken by emotion, "I can't tell you how much I feel your love and kindness. You must not think me obstinate or proud, but I *can't* take your money. In truth, so long as grandfather Canonge lives, I want for nothing, and even the three hundred per annum is superfluous. I need very little now, though I have cost grandfather a great deal in travelling about, and experimenting with surgeons and doctors all over the world; but I have given it all up. My trip to Germany this past summer ended it. I have tried every thing, and gone everywhere, to everybody. It comes to nothing. The same old opinion reiterated again and again. They all say: 'At any moment it is possible the power to walk may return as suddenly as you lost it. But it must come from a rush of internal vital force. The paralyzed nerve cannot be reached by any external agent or remedy.'"

"You have tried electricity and every thing?" said Victor Burthe, interrogatively.

"And the faith doctor and mesmerism?" added Natika.

Mark smiled sadly. "I have tried every thing, however absurd, or superstitious, or scientific! What matters it to me *what* restores me, so I am restored?"

"Old Nana says you are 'conjured,'" said Natika, half smiling, half weeping, at Mark's sad tones.

"I wish it was really so," replied Mark, with a laugh. "There would be some hope of getting unconjured, even if I had to seek the Vaudoo queen herself."

"That would be Nana, then," said Natika. "She is the queen! She keeps a tame snake in the gourd, and feeds it on milk, Lizbette says. All the negroes believe in her power, and are dreadfully afraid of her."

"I shouldn't be afraid of Nana, that old hag," exclaimed Victor. "I should be more afraid of her friend and mistress, your elegant stepmother, Mrs. Frances Bolling, Mark. I don't know why, but I do dislike that woman!"

"Oh, no, Victor!" replied Mark. "My stepmother is not a bad woman. She has had no control over me since I was twelve years of age. You know grandfather Canonge took me soon after my father's second marriage, and this paralysis came on while I was at college. I went out to take a sleigh ride one cold winter's day, got upset, had inflammatory rheumatism, and have never walked since. That's the whole story."

"Mrs. Bolling was *there*, and nursed you while

you were ill," said Victor. "She is a bad woman, I think. I never believed in her, somehow; but I don't exactly know how she *could* put you into such a condition as this."

"She was extremely kind to me," said Mark, gravely. "Such expressions about her annoy me, Victor. I know how strong your prejudices are, and that you dislike my stepmother, so don't let us talk of her."

"She is very handsome, and extremely agreeable," said Natika. "I like her very much, though I have only seen her a few times, when I was here before on a visit to grandfather Canonge. I suppose she will come to see me soon, Mark."

"I suppose she will, Natika. I sent word to Mrs. Flanoy's family to-day that you were here."

"I have been here a week now," said Natika. "A whole week."

"A whole week," said Victor, mimicking her inflection of voice. "What an eternity for a Parisian belle to waste in this dull country! I wonder you survive it, Natika."

"I suppose decency requires of me to see my grandfather occasionally, Victor, as it also impels you to come and 'waste your sweetness on this desert air,' at least once in ten years, for a few days. Think of poor Mark having to live here *all* the time, and blush for your self-indulgence."

"The truth is, I am very soon bored in the

country," responded Victor. "I don't care much for shooting and fishing, and I like to talk to men better than to trees, and I had rather listen to Grisi and Mario than to bird-singing."

"And you had rather flirt with a pretty woman than to do any thing else," rejoined Natika.

"Yes, I believe, 'that's a true bill,' as the lawyers phrase it, Natika," replied Victor, gayly, casting an involuntary glance at his own reflection in the mirror opposite. Natika's quick eye caught the rapid glance of vanity. She clapped her hands lightly, as if encoring a favorite maestro at the opera house, laughing, as she exclaimed—

"Vive! vive! Monsieur Narcisse! You are a handsome fellow, Victor. You have the beautiful dark eyes of the Canonges, and their fine straight features; but so has Mark, and you have *not* got the intellect of the Bollings; and that makes a difference in the expression, though most women would not find that out."

"Pshaw, Natika," said Victor. "You can't make me jealous of Mark, so you need not try that game, Miss Flash."

"Miss Flash! What is that?" asked Mark, smiling at the rencontre of his cousins.

"Oh, a sobriquet that the Americans in Paris gave to Natika," Victor said, carelessly. "She is so capricious and scintillating and brilliant in her ways and conversation."

Natika bit her lip—then she laughed, but there was no heartiness in the laugh. "Don't be stupid, Victor. I don't mind ill nature, but I can't bear stupidity. It bores me, especially in the country.

"Mark," she continued, throwing herself gracefully upon the lounge near his chair, picking up her poodle and fondling it, as she reclined on the soft cushions; "Mark, what has become of that frightful boy of your stepmother's?—her son by the first marriage? What was his name?"

"Antony Coolidge, do you mean?" asked Mark.

"Yes."

"He is still at St. Louis practising law, I believe. He comes here sometimes to see his mother."

"He was a *very* ugly boy," remarked Natika. "He had real African features, though he had blue eyes and sandy hair. He looked like a white negro—"

"So he is," interrupted Victor. "I beg your pardon, Mark, but every body knows that Mrs. Bolling was only the natural half-sister of Major Flanoy. Old Governor Flanoy acknowledged her, and, according to the French law, legitimized her. But her mother was a quadroon, you know, so Antony Coolidge is only a reversion, according to the natural law of Genesis, to the original type of his grandmother's race. It is *atavism*."

Mark frowned, but did not contradict the statement of Victor. He knew it to be true.

"I like pure blood," said Natika, "even in my dogs. Fanfan is a highly bred poodle. See how delicate she is." And she held up the poodle's paw.

"You forget, Natika," said Mark, quietly, "that the Bollings are descendants of Pocahontas. So that *I* have a strain of Indian in *my* blood."

"Oh, that's very different!" said Natika. "I don't dislike such a strain as that. It is such a different race of people."

"You know they say now there was no such person as the Princess Pocahontas," put in Victor.

"No such person as Mrs. Harris," said Natika, laughingly.

Mark's handsome face crimsoned, as he replied, haughtily—

"I suppose we know best who are her descendants."

"I should think you ought to," said Victor, lightly. "I don't quarrel with history or tradition. I take it as it is told to me. I believe in *all* of it. In Napoleon and Pocahontas, and Captain John Smith and Villere's bloody shirt, and *every thing, enfin.*"

"What a remarkably developed phrenological organ of credulity!" said Natika.

"Well! I have to accept the alternative of believing every thing or believing nothing, and the former state is the pleasantest, so I adopt it," replied Victor, sitting himself down upon the footstool by

Natika's sofa. "I don't even doubt *you*, Natika, when you tell me you never coquette, and are never inconstant to *nos premiers amours*."

Natika made a " mou " at him.

" If you do that again I shall kiss you, Natika," said Victor, resolutely. " I have as good a right to kiss you as Mark has." And there came a sudden vivid flash in Victor's eyes.

" No ! you haven't, because you are not so good as Mark," replied Natika. "And besides"—she paused—

"And besides," repeated Victor, looking sharply at her.

"And besides," continued Natika, smoothing her dog's silken ears, " I am not as fond of you as I am of my cousin Mark," and she glanced at him defiantly.

Victor looked steadily at her. Her eyes did not fall. She looked as steadily back into his.

"Don't try to make a *heros de Roman* of yourself, Victor," she remarked. " It is purely absurd and a great waste of ' matériel !' "

" I know you think so, Natika," Victor replied. " Mark," he continued, turning to Mark, who had been sitting with his hand over his eyes, apparently unconscious of the by-play of talk between his cousins, "Mark, what has become of Major Flanoy's only daughter, that little white creature—nearly an Albino—that used to come here so often, prowling about you ?"

"Who? Major Flanoy's daughter?" asked Mark, starting up to a more erect position in his chair and dropping his hand from his eyes.

"Oh, you mean Panola. Yes, she was very fair. She is grown up now."

> "Her hair it was lint-white,
> Her skin it was snow-white,
> Bright was the flash of her blue, rolling e'e,"

sang Victor, remodelling Burns to suit his own ideas; then he went on:

"She was uncanny, Mark, that child. She was so white altogether."

"Therefore she was justly named PANOLA," said Mark.

"What does that mean?" asked Natika. "It is a queer name."

"It means 'cotton,'" replied Mark. "It is the Indian name for cotton. Mrs. Flanoy is a half-breed Cherokee, one of the Ross family. Major Flanoy was in the army, stationed on the frontier of the Indian Nation. He married his wife there. She was very pretty, and well educated at Mrs. Willard's school in Troy. The major got most of his fortune by her—she was rich. Panola is their only child; therefore an heiress."

"What a singular family those Flanoys must be! so much miscegenation among them," observed Natika.

"They are peculiar, or rather were, since they are

all dead now except Panola and her mother. The major died last year. The old governor must have had a fearful temper. He died from breaking a bloodvessel in a fit of rage."

"Is this creature—this Albino, as Victor calls her—like them, or like her Indian ancestors?" asked Natika, yawning in a suppressed well-bred way, as she pushed her poodle off her lap and sat upright on the sofa.

"She is like—" began Mark, when the door was suddenly thrown open, and a servant entered, announcing "Miss Flanoy, Master Mark."

CHAPTER II.

THE HEROINE.

VICTOR BURTHE sprang up from his low seat at Natika's feet, and bowed instinctively as the young girl entered the door. Panola paused for an instant, struck aback at the unexpected sight of strangers in Mark's private sitting-room; for, though she was aware that Mark's cousins were guests of Docteur Canonge at this time, the servant had awkwardly conducted her, without notification, into their presence.

3

It was only an instant that Panola hesitated; but that was long enough for Natika and Victor, with their practised eyes of society, to take an inventory of her charms. The quick dilation of Victor's eyes, and the sudden compressure of Natika's full, red lips, showed surprise, and, in one of them, vexation, at the vision suddenly presented to their well-bred but rather insolent gaze. "Resplendence of beauty," thought Victor. "Where's the little Albino?"

"What a complexion!" thought Natika.

The first impression Panola induced was a perception of perfect bodily healthfulness. No young Spartan maiden, dancing before Parthenope, was ever more symmetrical in form, more graceful in her poses, than was Panola. In the picturesque words of her mother's people, "Panola was straight as a young ash tree; flexible as the reed by the river's side; her skin was white as a cotton-flake; her lips were red as the berries of the *fire-tree;* her eyes were blue as the waters of the great lakes; her hair was golden as the silk of the maize; her cheeks were pink as the sunset clouds; she walked with the lightness of the panther and the swiftness of the red deer; her form had the graceful swaying motion of the wind-waved, gray moss upon the trees of the forest, and when she laughed, it was like the silver sounds of falling waters." This was the description of Panola that "Cherokee Joe" gave once to his chief, her mother's cousin, the great Satana. Victor thought it was a very pretty tableau, as Panola stood motionless, with the intense quiescence of an Indian, for a moment in the doorway.

Panola was dressed very simply. A gown, cut à la Gabrielle, fitted close to her perfect figure. She wore a scarf of brilliant blue stuff, pinned squarely around her shoulders, more in the fashion of an Indian blanket than in the usual style of a Scotch plaid. The gold brooch, which held the square blue mantle in position, was made into the *totem* of her mother's family. It was a capital imitation, in enamel of black and gold, of a coiled rattlesnake, with head thrust out to strike. The snake's eyes were of large diamonds; its tongue encrusted with small rubies; they glittered fiercely in the sun rays. Panola wore a jaunty little hat, trimmed with blue ribands, surmounted by the plumes from the wings of the white crane, and these delicate feathers were fastened in place by an aigrette, similar to her snake brooch, of gold and diamonds. The two snakes seemed almost alive, they were so admirable in workmanship. She had on gloves of pearl-gray kid, and her little, highly-arched feet, set straight on her path as she walked, were fitted with tiny bronzed boots, *without heels*, of Tournelle's finest make. She walked swiftly, straight and noiselessly, as her ancestors did when they slipped lightly through the pathless forests, ages and ages before her coming.

Panola held a small basket in one hand, and she

carried a gold-mounted driving-whip in the other. She caught Victor's eye and his glance of admiration. She smiled and nodded her small head in sudden recognition, saying frankly, "Mr. Burthe, how do you do? I have not forgotten you, though I suspect you have forgotten me; I was such a little child when we last met. I am glad to see you again."

Victor sprang forward with outstretched hand, eager to claim the friendly recognition. But Panola only smiled and nodded gayly as she passed by him towards Mark.

"Panola, my cousin, Miss Jacquimin," said Mark, in his chair, waving his hand towards Natika.

Panola walked forward without pausing, deposited her whip and basket on the table by Mark's side; then, turning quite deliberately to Natika, putting her hands together before her, made a profound and deep courtesy, à l'Espagnolle. It took quite a minute to perform the reverence. The Spanish queen herself never made it more slowly and more gracefully.

"She has had a dancing-master, at any rate," thought Natika, as she half rose and bowed with careless Parisian grace to this strange girl.

"She wouldn't shake hands," thought Victor Burthe.

Mark knew that Panola never did offer her hand to any one whom she did not specially love;

she was very chary of any personal demonstration towards any one. A clasp of the hand meant a great deal from Panola.

She positively rejected the small insincerities of society. She was always singularly true, but coldly polite to strangers. She rarely ever showed surprise or astonishment at anything—very different in that from her present companions, who were full of French vivacity, and were continually "taking fire," old Docteur Canouge said, "at things and people."

Natika looked amused as she caught Victor's eye.

Victor could not repress a smile, in spite of his French courtesy; but Panola paid no further attention to the cousins. She turned to Mark, handing him the small basket wreathed with fresh passion-flowers.

"Mark, here are some fine pomegranates that I kept in the greenhouse to ripen for you. See the pretty red seeds bursting through the rinds; and here's a bunch of monockanock lilies. Aren't they sweet? I went out on the lake in my dug-out, this morning, to gather them myself."

"They are lovely, Panola," said Mark, extending his hand for the basket. He took out its treasures one by one.

"Passion-flowers, ripe pomegranates, at this season too; and monocka blooms, sweet as the giver, Panola."

Panola laughed like a pleased child. " I like to please you, Mark," she said, frankly, without affectation.

Panola had the low silvery laugh as well as the flute voice of the Indian woman. Mr. Ruskin says that it requires " generations of culture and refinement to render a voice sweet in speech;" where, then, do Indian women get their proverbially soft, lovely voices and laughter from?

" Victor, Natika, have a pomegranate!" exclaimed Mark. " Panola, won't you hand the basket to my cousins, as I can't?"

Panola took up the basket instantly, and carried it silently and swiftly—her motions were all swift and quiet—offering the fruit first to Natika, then to Victor. Natika took a pomegranate. Victor took the basket from Panola to replace it on the table.

" No," said Panola, " no; take the fruit. Mark wished *me* to serve you. I serve my *friends* with pleasure."

Mark laughed. " And what would you do to your enemies, Panola?"

" I have none," she replied; " but if I had—" she paused.

" Well, if you had?" asked Mark.

" I do not know; I am part *Cherokee.*"

Victor thought Natika made a very pretty picture, as she sat eating her red pomegranate seeds, teasing Faufan by offering the fruit to her occasionally. Fanfan sniffed at the seed, shaking her curly ears in disgust. Natika had all the grace of a Cypriote and all the ease of a Parisienne.

"Take care, Natika! you will stain your fingers with that rind!" exclaimed Victor. "What an absurdity it is to talk of the romance of the pomegranate groves in Moorish Spain! They planted the groves so as to make tannin for their leather from the rinds—Cordovan leather. Your finger-tips will be tanned, Natika."

"I know very well how to eat a pomegranate, Victor. I sha'n't stain my fingers. I have not forgotten everything I ever knew before going to Paris!"

"I thought you *had*," said Victor.

"Mark," said Panola, as she replaced the basket of fruit by his side, "aunt Bolling bade me say she was prevented from calling to-day upon Miss Jacquimin, on account of the arrival of Antony. But she will hope to have that pleasure to-morrow."

"Has Antony come?" inquired Mark.

"Yes; he arrived to-day from St. Louis. We did not expect him," said Panola, indifferently. "I should have been over to see you before, Mark, but mamma has been so unwell and so suffering this week that I could not leave her until this afternoon, when she is sleeping, with Isobel to watch by her. She was so ill that she sent a letter to the Nation by Cherokee Joe to her cousin, the chief Sataua. Joe returned to-day and brought back the reply to mamma's letter. She seemed so restless until it came; but then she got quiet and satisfied, and went to sleep."

"Is the chief coming here?" asked Mark, with interest; "I should like to see him."

"I did not understand; I did not see the letters. Joe wrote mamma's in Cherokee, at her dictation. I was not present. The reply was in the same tongue. I speak it, of course, it being my mother's tongue; but I don't write it very well, it is so difficult. I can spell out a simple sentence. It has no literature except translations from English and other tongues, you know."

"Yes, I know," said Mark; "but it was a remarkable people that could invent an alphabet and a written tongue of their own."

"Yes; Sequoyah was a great man," replied Panola, a bright flush of pleasure gliding over her face and neck as she spoke. Victor thought she was prettier now than Natika; but just then Natika moved into a still more graceful attitude, and Victor remained as undecided in opinion as Paris was once.

"Natika's father was Greek," said Mark. "She writes and speaks Romaic as well as English. Victor is all French Creole, and I am half French and half English, with a strain of Indian blood in me."

"And *I* am part Cherokee, and my father's father

was a pure Netherlander," said Panola. "What a mixture of races there is in America!"

"*My* race is not mixed," said Natika, haughtily; "nor Victor's either. You can't call Greek and French a mixture of races. They are both Aryan in origin."

"Not so certain," said Mark, seeing the flash in Panola's eye, and hastening to forestall any strife between his guests. "M. Quatrefages declares that the French are not Aryan in origin."

"I don't believe in M. Quatrefages," said Natika, pettishly. "Victor, it is lovely in the garden. Let us go out for a walk, if Miss Flanoy and Mark will be so good as to excuse us for a little while."

Panola and Mark eagerly assured Natika of their entire willingness to excuse them; so Natika called to Fanfan to follow her, threw a white scarf around her shoulders, and, nodding "au revoir" to Panola and Mark, she stepped out of the open French window on to the verandah, and thence into the well-kept flower-garden. Victor followed her, not altogether pleased, but true to his old allegiance. Natika had ruled him since he was twelve years of age: indeed, Natika had moulded Victor's character. She was two years older than he, and much more intelligent, and had a stronger will. When Victor was with her she controlled him most despotically; when separated from her he was sometimes rather rebellious; but a line or a word would bring the truant

back to her feet at any moment. Natika's power was a
fascination that Victor could never resist, any more
than a trained falcon can resist the call of the
whistle and the waving of the jessies. He belonged
to the *animum revertend;* the domesticated game
which must return to its owner. He had asked
Natika to marry him about twice in every week
since he was grown up to years of majority, and had
been as often rejected by her. But her rejections
were so softened by her natural coquetry, that Victor had never been able to reduce his hopes to absolute despair. Sometimes he would get angry and
go away from Natika for months; once he stayed
away for nearly a year; then one day he reappeared
unexpectedly before her when she was "having a
very good time" in Paris under the chaperonage of
some French friends—family connections of the
Canonges. Natika was not at all afraid of ever
losing her power over Victor: she whistled him back
whenever she wanted him. She loved power; she
did not love Victor; but she did not wish to lose his
devotion and homage; it was convenient for her, and
the close relationship gave her an unlimited opportunity to treat him exactly as she chose—sometimes
with tender affection, sometimes with cold indifference. Natika was that sort of a woman who is always
attractive to ordinary men, and she had usually a
small crowd of adorers, chiefly very young men,
who were dazzled by her vivacity, her wit, her

intelligence, and her money—for Natika was rich: she had thirty thousand dollars per annum in her own right, and now she was to receive this addition from uncle Jacob's will. Truly Natika was scarcely to blame if she felt as if she had the world in a sling, to cast her throw where she pleased.

Natika was twenty-seven years old now, and time will tell even on the fairest face; so she did feel a pang of jealousy as she confronted the fresh youth and beauty of the seventeen-year-old Panola. Still she had great advantages over Panola. She was an accomplished woman of the world, with all her variety of fascinations; and Panola was utterly simple and unformed in manner; indeed Panola was less wise about social usages than young girls generally are, because her nature was partly that of the Indian. She was straightforward, plain and unpretending, with much of the impassive quiet which she inherited from her mother. When she was in society she rarely spoke, unless some one spoke to her. She never volunteered an opinion, or a graceful jest or witticism, as her French friends continually did; she did not understand how to make a conversation. What she had to say she said modestly, but earnestly and firmly. She sat usually in a state of utter immobility, except for the quick restless glancing of her blue eyes, which allowed nothing to escape their rapid gaze. She talked more freely to Mark Bolling than to any other human being; even her mother, a quiet Indian in manner, never had received the confidences Panola gave to Mark, who understood her perfectly. He could almost read her thoughts at times; and he loved her intensely, with a love of utter self-abnega- tion and of despair. He had watched the gradual transformation of the pale, snow-white child into this exquisitely lovely maiden. He had helped to develop her slowly-maturing mind, until it seemed to him as if the very wine and the sunshine of life had grown to be incarnated in the body of Panola. She brought fresh vitality, and the actual presence of health and joy to him whenever she approached him. A Swedenborgian would have said the emanations of Panola's sphere were all life-giving, they were so pure and so wholesome. If Panola had any "nerves," she did not know it. Natika was full of nerves, and sentimental fancies. Panola had a quiet contempt for Natika and for all such weak fine ladies. Mark knew this instinctively, and he was glad to be left alone with Panola, while Natika and Victor walked in the garden.

CHAPTER III.

A FAMILY GROUP.

PANOLA knelt down by Mark's chair soon as the cousins disappeared out of the apartment. She took Mark's hand and held it, smoothing it with hers as she said:

"Mark, you look troubled. What has occurred? Tell Panola."

Mark could never resist the pleading tones of Panola's voice; so he had to tell her all about uncle Jacob's will.

Panola listened attentively; her tender, soft touches comforted Mark. He leaned back in his chair with his eyes closed; but his expression of countenance showed that the worst bitterness of his disappointment was over, now that he was sure of Panola's sympathy. He did not dare trust himself to look at Panola: he knew that his glances would alarm and startle her childlike confidence in him. So he shut his eyes while she held his hand so lovingly; and he did not even clasp her fingers; he let his hand lay supinely in her cool, soft palms. Every pulse throbbed and bounded, and a lover's joy flowed to the innermost recesses of his heart; but Mark controlled himself by an imperious strength of will; he did not allow a tremor:

he braced himself internally and sat as if he were turned into stone. He could not risk the loss of Panola's affectionate friendship, which was so much to him in the impoverishment of his daily life.

"Mark," said Panola, after hearing all he had to tell, listening for the thousandth time to his plaintive laments over his useless existence, "Mark, why should your life be useless? You have studied medicine a good deal; why don't you help your grandfather in his practice? You could. Plenty of these poor 'gumbo French' and 'cajeaus' would be glad to come to you for consultation. I would not fret and grieve over myself. I would *make* occupation! It is not manly to repine."

Mark opened his eyes and looked at Panola.

"You are right, Panola," he replied. "You are always right; and you always do me good, Panola."

"I am glad I do, dear Mark," said the girl, quite simply. "I think how much better off you are than poor mamma. Oh, Mark! it is too sorrowful to see mamma She is becoming so helpless now. She has lost now the use of her arms and hands. Her whole frame is rigid, except her head. Such a strange affection as it is! The doctors say they have never seen anything like it. She has never had a stroke of paralysis so far as she knows, and she is not affected like a paralytic; there is no withering nor change in her flesh. She is as round and plump as ever, and all the processes of the system seem to be perfect and unchanged. She never has had the least pain; but three years ago the joints of her toes became rigid, and gradually this rigidity has extended until now she lies as helpless as a body of stone. She is not affected as you are, Mark. You had rheumatic fever to cause your partial paralysis; but mamma has never had anything the matter with her, and she is not at all a nervous person."

"No," said Mark, "she is rather phlegmatic, and self-controlled as a stoic; she is not at all emotional."

"She is so reticent, too," continued Panola. "I have to guess at her feelings. She rarely expresses what she thinks or feels in words."

"But she has a firm will," said Mark, "quiet and undemonstrative as she is. Has she ever got over her prejudice against my stepmother?

"No, indeed, she has not. You know, long before papa died, mamma wouldn't suffer aunt Bolling to enter her room. It excited her so much that papa had to ask aunt not to go there. It troubled papa greatly; he was very fond of aunt Bolling. When he died, you know he requested in his will that she should be allowed to live in the Pavilion as long as it should be convenient for her to do so; and he left her half of his personal property. It was not much. The property was all mamma's, bought with her paraphernal money, and of course, by the laws of this State, papa could not dispose of it. The chief, Satana, had a contract of marriage drawn by the first lawyers of the State before he would consent to mamma's marriage with a white man."

"What reasons does your mother give for disliking my stepmother so intensely?"

"None, but that she does not like her; an Indian reason, you will think, Mark," laughed Panola. "But you know what an Indian's prejudices are—instinctive, I suspect; when they hate, they hate."

"And when they love, they are faithful unto death," said Mark, softly.

"Yes, we never forget a good; we never forgive an injury," said Panola, and a dark look came over her fair face, changing all its brightness like the passing of a cloud across the moon's disc. "You will think me very wicked, Mark. I am rather a pagan by organization, I believe sometimes. At any rate I feel much more sympathy with the old Stoics, whose books we read together, than I do with the Christian Scriptures. I believe, on occasion, I could see my enemy scalped or burnt at the stake, with as much satisfaction as my progenitors on the maternal side. Then, again, I am ashamed of such ferocity; that is, when the temperament of the Netherlanders is in the ascendant; then I think I could forgive my enemy and give him aid, and I love Christ and Christian teachings."

"It is the dual nature in you which makes this strife, Panola. At the end of your life you will see which has gained the victory; not before."

"I hope it may be the good Christian. I don't know, though."

"Does my stepmother reciprocate your mother's ill-will?" asked Mark, pursuing his train of thought.

"No; that's the worst of it! Aunt Bolling is so kind and so amiable, it makes me really uncomfortble. She is always ready to do any little thing for mamma, and often does, without mamma's knowing anything about it. She will go even into the kitchen and make the nicest jellies and daintiest cakes with her own hands, things that mamma is very fond of; and Isobel and I have to take them in and not let mamma know who it is that prepares them so deliciously. No one could be kinder than aunt Bolling."

"I have always found her very kind," said Mark, thoughtfully. "She was very good to me when she came to college and found me ill there. I have not been much with her. My father seemed to be fond of her. I have heard that she was very unhappy in her first marriage with Antony Coolidge's father. But they lived in Kentucky during their marriage; he was a citizen of that State. My father met her here, you know, whilst she was on a visit to her brother, Major Flanoy. They lived then in another

4

parish, and I was off at school and college under the care of grandfather Canonge; so I never saw her again until I was ill at college, and then here afterwards, when I found her domiciliated with Major Flanoy, after my father's sudden death."

"She always speaks very affectionately of you," said Panola. "She often wishes her own son was as good as you are, and I am sure I wish he was anything at all like you; for, as he is now, he is excessively disagreeable to me. I have to treat him politely, of course, on account of aunt Bolling; but I almost hate Antony Coolidge. I should like to stick arrows into him and burn him up, as my Cherokee great-great-grandmother would have done to anybody she did not like."

"I think, Panola," said Mark, smiling at the exaggeration of her expressions of antipathy, "that my stepmother has some views different from yours on that subject. She would like to draw the bonds of relationship closer between you and your half-cousin."

"Well, she'll never do it," said Panola, energetically, "for, if I do hate any human being, it is my half-cousin, Antony."

Just then their conversation was interrupted by hearing Victor Burthe's magnificent baritone voice ringing out the verse of Burns—he was teasing Natika about Panola's beauty—

" Her hair it is lint-white,
  Her skin it is milk-white,
Bright is the glance of her blue, rolling e'e ;
  Red, red, are her ripe lips,
  And sweeter than roses.
Oh ! where could my true love wander frae me ? "

"Oh, what a beautiful, beautiful voice!" ex- claimed Panola, starting to her feet and holding her head forward in an eager, listening attitude.

Mark smiled sadly at her impulsive movement. She had dropped his hand so quickly when the first note fell upon her ear.

"Victor's voice is very fine," he said. "He is considered to be the very finest baritone in New Orleans, that city of music."

"Oh, it is!" said Panola, with a half-sigh. "I wish he would sing some more."

"I will make him sing for you when he comes in," said Mark. "But here comes grandfather," he con- tinued, seeing the door open suddenly.

"Ah! Mademoiselle Panola," cried Docteur Ca- nonge, before he was well in the room, " I haf jus' receive' the notiss of your presence here. You bring wiz you ze beautiful sunshine! It haf been wedder not so good since here you was the week past. Mark and I, we haf missed you much; ver' great deal. I, more as Mark. He not haf so much galanterie as his ole granfader. Pauvre garçon ! "

The old docteur kissed Panola's hand, patted Mark on the shoulder, then drew a very snuffy, red silk

pocket-handkerchief out and blew his nose violently.
Panola saw the twinkling of a tear-drop in the old
man's eye, as he turned hastily away. He was
making an effort to hide his emotion, so as not to let
Mark see how troubled he was about the will.

He turned back to Panola. "You haf come now
in ver' good hour, in ver' best of time! for I haf
now, you see, my granddaughter, Natika, and my
grandson, Victor Burthe. You haf see Natika?
Ah, that is good, ver' good. An' you haf see
Victor? That is also good. He haf fine voice,
haf Victor Burthe! ver' fine! You shall hear him
sing. He sing be-eu-tifool! be-eu-teefool!" The
old docteur prolonged the adjective with a circumflex
accent upon it, opening his eyes widely, and spreading out his hands as he spoke it emphatically.

Panola assured him she fully credited all he said.
She had "heard Mr. Burthe sing a few notes
already."

"Ah! you haf him already hear? Ah, that is
well. But you haf not yet Natika hear declaim.
She haf fine talent, almost like mine, for de drame.
She ack well; presque comme Rachel. Her Hermione is ver' like Rachel. Ah! ma foi, you shall
see her. We shall haf soirée of charades and leetle
drame. Quelques declamations from Natika, and
some song from Victor, and some belle musique
from you; you will bring de Stradinarius dat you
procure from Mexique, and you will play for us;

and Mark shall listen, an' shall play at cartes wid some friends of de voisin; and I shall ack in charades, and we shall have cotillon, and I shall dance wid Madame Duplessis, la mère Nicolline, and also wid you, Mademoiselle Panola, and wid de veuve charmante, Madame votre tante. You can come demain; to-morrow, perhaps. I will consulte wid Natika, and wid Lizbette. Lizbette *muss* be consulte, you know, Mademoiselle Panola"—the gay old man nodded his head and laughed—"Lizbette rule Mark and I. We ver' much fear Lizbette! N'este ce pas, Mark?"'

Mark smiled. "Yes, indeed, grandpapa! Lizbette would revenge herself by giving us cold coffee and burnt toast if we didn't consult her in all domestic arrangements. You had better ask her first, before you invite any of your guests."

"I tink so, indeed. I shall go immediatement to consulte Lizbette. You stay, Mademoiselle Panola, jusqu'à mon retour from de Tartarean region; Orphée will soon return," and the merry old man darted out of the room like a superannuated swallow, swiftly, if rather tremulously—singing, in a cracked falsetto and in very quavering style, as he went:

"Que faro senza, Eurydice."

He was very quaint in appearance, as thin as a human being could be, with a fine, cleanly-cut, delicate, long French countenance, not very wrinkled, but very pale and sallow. His head was good; his forehead very intellectual; his dark eyes, bright and sparkling, beamed with good nature and vivacity. His eyebrows and hair were very white. He wore a four-cornered skull-cap of black velvet. He was very neatly dressed in the summer costume of striped blue linen, worn by Creoles in Louisiana. His hands were small, the fingers long and delicate, the thumb and forefinger of his right hand slightly stained from the use of snuff.

He soon returned with Lizbette's gracious permission for the soirée, which he announced triumphantly to Panola, then running to the Venetian door, he called out as loudly and shrilly as possible:

"Natika! Victor! Venez ici mes cheres enfans! As quick as possible! Come, my children! I am in much haste!"

Natika and Victor quickly obeyed their grandfather's summons. They came in great haste, almost out of breath. Natika was quite flushed with anxiety to know what was wanted. She had been absent from him so many years she had forgotten her grandfather's impulsive ways. She looked blankly at Victor, who, with his usual insouciance, shrugged his shoulders and laughed when Docteur Canonge announced his intention of having a soirée on the following evening. "He had already consulte Lizbette," he said. "She had gracieusement agree for to make grand efforts in ze way of gumbo fillet, also oystères and oder tings for un petit souper, and' Mademoiselle Panola she 'ave promis to assist wid her violin magnifique, and also, he was sure, would his dear children Natika and Victor give their amiable tributes to the recreations of the evening."

Victor recovered his self-possession sooner than Natika. Docteur Canonge was waiting impatiently for their approbation of his scheme of entertainment. Victor assured his grandfather that he might rely upon him for any amount of singing short of a whole opera, and Natika was compelled to adopt the rôle of graceful obedience, though she privately informed Victor she considered the whole affair would be a tremendous bore; an evening with country neighbors and home-made music not appearing very inviting to this spoiled belle of Parisian salons. "But at any rate it will be a novelty," she said. "I shall have you and Mark as a dernier resource when I grow weary of the campagnards."

Panola arose from her chair now to go home. Docteur Canonge darted forward to accompany her to her carriage. "Mademoiselle Panola," he said, "you will convey mes homages respecteuses, to your charming aunt, Madame Bolling, and to Monsieur Antony, votre cousin, and you will request them to honor me with their agreeable society to-morrow evening. Mark, you will write for me leetle notes to ze Smitts and ze Clark familles, as I do not so

good English write as you. I will myself send un
billet to die famille Duplessis—all zie four familles
of zem—particulierement Madame Duplessis mère."

The merry little docteur talked all the way out
of the room, as he walked by Panola's side, out of
the hall, on to the verandah, and to the front gate,
where her phaeton was in waiting, with a man on
horseback to accompany it. Victor followed to put
Panola into her carriage.

"Mademoiselle Panola," said the old docteur,
lowering his voice cautiously, "you see my poor
Mark is ver' much trouble. You have heard of that
villain will? That testament malin of my brudder
Jacob? Ah! si ingrat and malicieux of Jacob!
Zu mock dat boy so! He cut me off wid nozing!
précisément nozing! and he give Mark ver' leetle.
I am ver' glad he gif so much zu Natika and zu
Victor; but it is hard for poor Mark! His fader
gif him nozing cider! Madame Bolling sa veuve
charmante she get what Bolling had; not much!
I haf got some leetle, and I will gif to Mark all I
can; but it is ver' sad for poor Mark, and I will
have soirée pour égayer Mark! and for compliment zu Natika and zu Victor," ended the courteous docteur, catching sight of Victor behind them.

Victor smiled, and walked faster up to Panola's
other side. He had overheard his grandfather.

Panola assured the dear old man that she would
do all in her power to second his good intentions,

and she shook hands with him as he assisted her into her phaeton. Victor stood idly by. Panola did not offer her hand, but bowed to him politely. The groom mounted his horse. Panola touched her ponies with her whip, and was soon whirled away, leaving Docteur Canonge and Victor leaning on the low gate gazing after her.

"That's Cherokee Joe wiz Mademoiselle Panola," said Docteur Canonge. "He always ride after her; but never after no one else. He only hunt and shoot and keep zie larder supply wiz game for Major Flanoy; but he go wiz Panola whenever she go alone. Her fader dead and her moder sick. I expect die chief Satana make Joe stay to look after Panola. If anybody do harm to Panola all zie tribe of zie Cherokees would hunt him down. Zose Injuns never forgives nor forgets any ting good—neider bad."

"I shouldn't like to have the hatred of an Indian," observed Victor, lightly, "especially of a whole tribe of Cherokees! Do you think, grandpapa, they can ever be civilized entirely?"

"As a pure race, no! I zink zey are as essentially savage as zie wolf! But as zie wolf may be metamorphose graduellement, into zie faithful dog, so zie Indian may be changed by zie mingling of blood wiz zie white races."

"But you do not approve of any mixture of races, grandpapa?"

"No! Zie white races have attained zeir excellence through much effort, and in course of long ages of time. Not only zie volume, but zie *quality* of zeir brain matter is zie result of activities, experiences, sufferings, perhaps, to which no oder race of man has been subjected. I do not very willingly see zat jeopardized; but of all zie colored races, zie Indian of America is least objectionable. He possesses some very fine traits of nature, which in zie best specimens of hybrids among zem, are quite admirable! But dere are Indians and Indians! Among zie savage races of man, as in zie savage races of beasts, zere are lions and tigers and panthers, and also *jackals*. I admire zie lions; I do not particularly like zie jackal."

"Do you think they can ever be made into good citizens, grandpapa?"

"I doubt it! We must put away all zie romantic notions about zose Indians. Zey are a strong race. A people different from all oders. Can you tame wholly zie tiger or zie zebra? zie onagra? Can you make zie rattlesnake gentle? If you can, den you may hope to tame zie unmixed Indian. Zey are brave, proud, continent, stoical, strong, but zey are deceitful as zie adder, cunning as zie wildcat, persevering, obstinate, suspicious, revengeful, and quick-sighted as zie lynx. What can you do wiz such a people? Change his blood or kill him. Zat is all we can do. I do not myself expect to see zic catamount and zic jaguar ploughing zic fields, instead of zic ox or zic mule."

NOTE.—Their religion is a sort of Theism. They believe in a Great Spirit who governs all things, and they believe, like the Persians, in an evil spirit, which they call "Ah-skeen-er." He is an invisible spirit, who is not susceptible of a good thought, and whose tendency is essentially *always* in favor of *evil*, and that he has innumerable other *subordinate* evil spirits, subject to his influence and bidding, that continually infest the earth and all things connected therewith (including the air), and which are never idle in their *inspirations* of evil to the human family as well as to the brute creation. Hence all the evil passions are generally, by the Cherokees, charged to the Devil—or, as they call him in their native language, "*Ah-skeen-er*," which signifies the *quintessence of meanness*. Also, misfortunes, accidents of injurious character, sickness, bad dreams, evil forebodings, mental aberration, etc., are supposed to be the work of devils, who obey the will of their great master, the chief of *all* devils, whose throne or chief-seat is generally conceded to be somewhere in the next world, opposite the "Happy hunting-grounds," and in a region where the sun never shines, and where total darkness prevails, and where *briars* and *thorns* grow *densely all over the country*, and the game is always *wild*. The devil receives the wicked (or those to be punished for their bad work on this earth) from the hands of his *executive* officers (the subordinate devils already alluded to) and turns them loose, in this cheerless region, *naked* and *hungry*. The punishment in this Cherokee *Hell* appears to be, that the parties punished do not and cannot know each other, on account of the darkness, but are in *mutual* fear of each other; that, being always famished or hungry, they are in continual but vain pursuit of the *wild* game, and that being *naked*, their persons are continually torn by the *briars* and *thorns* that cover the country. These, I think, are substantially the outlines of the Cherokee idea of the *prince* of devils and his "imps."

CHAPTER IV.

ACTED CHARADES.

FATE was propitious to Docteur Canonge—the evening was clear and bright, and all his guests accepted *avec plaisir*. They came before dark. The salons were thrown open and were well lighted with lamps and candles. The long, one-storied house, with the wide verandahs in front and back, made quite a brilliant display, as the guests drove up in their various equipages. Madame Bolling, Antony and Panola came in a handsome close coach, with outriders, one of whom was Cherokee Joe, mounted upon a little black Indian pony. The Smith and Clark families had already arrived, and Docteur Canonge was trying to amuse them with some stereoscopic views, that Mark had collected during his travels in search of health. The Smiths and the Clarks were Americans, recently moved into the neighborhood. They were good, commonplace, rather stiff and awkward, people, fearful to entertain, for, as Docteur Canonge whispered to Panola, "*they were not at all responsive in character.*"

Natika had begun to look as patiently resigned as St. Catherine, a martyr on her wheel; Victor was good-naturedly trying to talk to the eldest Miss Clark, who professed to be musical, and promised

" to execute the Glenmary waltzes in the course of the evening." Mr. Clark was a tall, slab-sided man, with a hooked nose, who talked so rapidly, and cut off his words in such a manner, that Docteur Canonge, with his imperfect knowledge of English, found him, as he told Panola, " *enormously difficult to comprehend.*" Madame Clark (as she was much pleased to be called—it sounded grander than plain Mrs.) was " enormously " fat, and rather jolly ; she laughed and was in a good humor with everything and everybody. The Smiths were languishing, drawling, and fashionably indifferent about everything ; there were three young ladies of them ; their mamma, who wore caps trimmed with red ribbons and yellow flowers ; and also there was a brother, who was an exquisite, sporting yellow gloves, who carried an eye-glass, and wished to devote himself to Natika, whom he decided immediately " to be stunning."

Docteur Canonge darted forward to meet Madame Bolling and her party. He was immensely relieved at their arrival. The Smiths and Clarks were almost too much for him. Madame Bolling entered leaning upon her son's arm ; Panola followed, and a servant came after her, carrying a small violin-box, which Panola carefully deposited herself in a very safe corner of an *étagère.* It contained her Straduarius, a violin, precious as gold or diamonds to a true artiste. Madame Bolling was handsome ; her eyes were

large and bright, but so black that there did not
seem to be any gradation of tinting between the
iris and pupil, which gave a singular expression to
them; her lashes were so long they curled upwards
like deep fringes, her nose was decidedly *retroussé;*
some persons, evil-minded, might have called it a
positive snub; it was rather spread out at the nos-
trils, showing the strain of African blood; the mouth
was large and sensuous, with full, rich, red lips, and
when she smiled she showed two rows of strong,
white teeth; her forehead was low; the black hair,
wavy and abundant, grew down nearly to her eyebrows, which were black and strongly marked; she
had a well-formed, shapely figure, rather inclined to
embonpoint; her hands were large, and thick in the
fingers.   She was elaborately dressed in a crimson-
satin gown, with lace flounces, her neck and arms
bare—they were fat and handsome; altogether she
was an attractive woman.

Antony Coolidge did not resemble his mother.
He was very homely, and, as Natika said, "he looked
like a white negro."   He had good manners, and
was quiet, but rather heavy in conversation.

Panola was dressed in white tarlatan (the usual
dress of young Louisiana girls); she had a blue
ribbon around her waist, and she wore her rattle-
snakes, one in her breast, and one in her hair made
the clasp of a wreath of forest leaves, and small,
white, well-opened cotton bolls which she wore

around her head; a fantastic but pretty crown, trying to any complexion but one so fair as Panola's.
Her long, straight hair, which looked like the spun,
yellow threads made by glass-blowers, was knotted
up and tied with a blue ribbon, low on the neck,
rather in Indian style than that of Monsieur Algée.
But it suited Panola. Natika looked at her with
curiosity; she considered her style decidedly "outrée"
and "sauvage."

All the families of the Duplessis now poured into
the room, and there began to be a clatter of tongues
and such an interchanging of compliments that the
whole roof commenced to echo and re-echo, and
Docteur Canonge's soirée was fairly started on a
prosperous and successful tide. A man, who had
been employed for the purpose, opened the piano
and began to play gay waltzes and dances. The
merry Duplessis were soon whirling around the
room, and everybody was very quickly drawn into
the vortex. Docteur Canonge led off the cotillon
with Madame Duplessis, mère, who was seventy
years old, and wore a turban of black lace, with a
bird of paradise fastened on the top of her gray hair.
She was a small, active old Frenchwoman, light as
a bird, and she danced down the cotillon with
twinkling feet and sparkling eyes. Her great-grand-
children were dancing too, and her granddaughter
and her granddaughter's husband. Her daughter
was playing cards with Mark "*at present.*"

Madame Bolling was led out by Mr. Clark, and Panola danced with Victor. Natika fell to the share of Antony Coolidge; she did not exert herself to be specially agreeable until she caught a glance of unequivocal admiration in his stupid, watery, blue eyes, and Natika was coquette enough to be pleased at anybody's admiration, so she began to rouse herself and to talk a little more.

The Duplessis flew about over the floor like so many sparrows. After the first cotillon they had some charades. Natika soon found that unpromising as had been the exterieur she was surrounded by first-rate native talent. All the Duplessis acted well. Docteur Canonge was really inimitable in his way. It was as good as a French vaudeville. Antony Coolidge had decent abilities as an actor. Madame Bolling was fine; so was Victor, and Natika found out she would have to exert all her talent to hold her own among them. Panola did not act well; she had not the gift of personation, but she was lovely in tableaux. So they made her into an Iphigenia at Aulis.

Docteur Canonge was the sacrificing priest; Victor was Achilles; Madame Bolling Clytemnestra; and a Judge Morgan, from Kentucky, who was a guest of the Smiths, and whom they had requested permission to bring to the soirée, was metamorphosed into a fine Agamemnon, with his head buried deep in Madame Bolling's black velvet circular, which answered very well for a classic mantle under the exigencies of the occasion. This tableau was en-cored repeatedly, and each time Docteur Canonge, the laurel-crowned priest, assumed a more ferocious aspect as he clasped the sacrificial knife, one of his largest surgical instruments, in his hand. Victor Burthe sang his very best after this. He watched Panola's face to see what she thought of his singing. He was flattered by her breathless attention. He glided to her side. "You are fond of music, Mademoiselle Panola!"

"*Fond* of music!' said Panola, opening her blue eyes widely. "I think sometimes *my life is in music.*"

"That's a strong expression," said Victor, smiling.

"I suppose it is," replied Panola.

Just then Docteur Canonge came to speak to Panola, and she went off with him. In a few mo-ments a low strain of music filled the salon.

It was a slow, solemn movement, and it seemed to Victor that there were at least four violins play-ing in perfect harmony. It had almost the effect of full orchestra. He looked at Mark for explana-tion. Mark smiled at his surprised glance.

"It is Panola," he whispered.

"Panola! does she play the violin like *that?*"

Mark nodded his head, but a stop was put to further conversation by the drawing back of the

5

curtains in front of the portion of the parlor impro-
vised into a stage.

Natika, in the classic drapery of Camille, with
young Duplessis as Horace, came forward. They
began to act scenes from Les Horaces of Corneille.
They were both good actors, and they warmed up
as they proceeded in their parts. At last they got
to the grand scene, where Horace brings in the
swords of the three Curiaces. Horace begins:

"Ma soeur voici le bras qui senge nos deux freres."

It was admirably rendered by Duplessis, but at
the close, where Camille makes the apostrophe to
",Rome," and ends with her fearful malediction,
Natika seemed literally inspired. Her small audience were electrified; her voice rang and thrilled
through every heart (she had studied from Rachel).
At the conclusion there was the greatest excitement;
the Duplessis clapped and stamped and cried "encore," and "bravo," until they were all hoarse.
Even the Smiths and Clarks caught the enthusiasm.
It was a moment of triumph for Natika; but at last
the curtain closed positively before her, and people
were beginning to subside into a little more quiet,
when Panola bounded out from behind the curtain,
dressed "as a young Bacchante," Docteur Canonge
said.

She had simply tied a tanned wolf's skin around
her shoulders, over her white frock, and put on a

pair of beaded Indian moccasins on her little feet, and tucked up her skirts rather short, and let her long, gold hair stream over her like a veil from under her crown of leaves. She looked "*wild*" enough, if rather an anachronism, as she sprang forth with her violin and bow in her hands and began to play the wildest, merriest tunes, flinging out the funniest and most grotesque combinations of notes. Everybody was suddenly seized with a fury of dancing; like the effect of the flute-player of the Tännenhauser, Panola's wild music seemed to set everybody crazy with fun.

Panola played jigs, reels, Highland flings, Italian tarantelles. Her bow seemed to fly like a gleam of light across the strings; at last she fell into the tune of the "Arkansas Traveller;" she played it in every key and with every modulation; she made it laugh, and cry, and whine, and jerk, and trill, and quiver; she played it single, and double, and triple, and quadruple. Everybody was dancing, and laughing like mad people, until Panola saw that they were absolutely exhausted, when gradually she toned her music down till it quietly died away. She disappeared suddenly behind the curtains again, and the weary dancers sunk upon their chairs breathless and gasping.

Mark had laughed till he cried, and sat now in his chair wiping off the traces of tears from his cheeks. His grandfather was very happy to see Mark laugh.

Lizbette announced the serving of the supper, and Panola reappeared, grave and demure, dressed again as she was in the early part of the evening. Lizbette's gumbo and oysters were perfect. "The mayonaise of red-fish and the salad" Docteur Canonge had prepared himself, he said; so they were beyond praise. Some cold roast turkey and a ham, with pâtés, little cakes, and confitures, and some delicious aspic jelly of white grapes, and oranges, bananas and pineapples, with plenty of excellent claret, a good cup of black coffee, and a pousse café of a thimbleful of curaçoa or strong Marischino, concluded the *ménu*. It was done full justice to, and after supper everybody made their obeisances to Natika, and thanked Docteur Canonge for their "delightful evening," and they all went home.

As Judge Morgan rode home with young Smith in his cabriolet he asked him about the different people they had met, especially Madame Bolling, about whom he seemed to have some curiosity. He had been introduced to her, and had danced with her, but by some accident had not been introduced to her son. He spoke of her now carelessly, but with evident interest. Smith knew very little about her, as it was the first time he had met any of the neighbors; his family had only recently moved here. He told Judge Morgan that "she was a half-sister of Major Flanoy, and the aunt of Panola."

The judge sat meditating. "She *can't* be the same person, I suppose," he said, at length, "else she would certainly have recognized *me* as I did her. She did not seem to know me at all ; but the woman I speak of *could* not have forgotten me. Oh, no ! that would be an impossibility. I never saw such a likeness in my life, though !"

"Where did you know anybody like Madame Bolling?" inquired Smith, roused at last into a faint curiosity.

"The woman I knew lived in ——," replied Morgan. "She was brought before me on a charge of lunacy, a charge preferred by her own husband ; but she came into court in her riding-habit, and stood up coolly in the box, tapping her little boot with her whip while the indictment was being read against her, and then, refusing the aid of any law-yer, she defended herself most eloquently. It was impossible to send her to an asylum. The jury gave the verdict in her favor without quitting their seats. Shortly after, the husband died, and she removed from the State. After her departure I heard a good many queer things about her, which rather puzzled me. She certainly was strange, and extremely cruel, I heard, to those in her power ; one of her slaves hung herself to escape from the tyranny and, some said, the torturing of her mistress. I don't know how true the facts were, but they were dreadful ; and if the woman was not insane, she was so wicked she should have been killed as one would destroy a noxious beast or reptile. They said she poisoned her husband, as well as other people. However, it was long ago, and Mrs. Coolidge is probably dead before this—"

"Mrs. Coolidge! Why, there was a young man there to-night named Coolidge. Did you not see him?" exclaimed Smith, wide awake now.

"No, I did not see him," said Judge Morgan, "but I am sorry I have to go off so early in the morning, else I should really like to meet that Madame Bolling again. She is a very handsome and interesting woman, very handsome, indeed! *very* handsome!"

"It was quite a success, Natika," exclaimed Victor, as the last of the guests departed. "Confess you have been often more bored in Madame Ronher's salons in Paris than at grandpapa's soirée to-night."

"Well, it wasn't so bad," replied Natika, with a yawn, "but I am very sleepy."

"The little cotton blossom is a wonder," said Victor. "Her music was like the bold

"Hearty rhymes,
New revived
Music of Acharnœ;
Choleric, fiery, quick
As the sparkle
From the charcoal

Of the native evergreen,
  Knotted oak
  In the smoke
Shows his active, fiery spleen,
Whilst beside
  Stands the dish
  Full of fish,
Ready to be fried."

Natika laughed. "Quote Aristophanes to a Greek in her own tongue, Victor, if you can!"

"Frere is very respectable," said Victor.

Docteur Canonge had caught the word "fish." So he said: "Oui, I sink de mayonaise *was* ver' good. I am glad you like him so much, Victor. I made him myself!"

CHAPTER V.

NATIKA JACQUIMIN.

THE father of Natika Jacquimin was a Greek, who came over on a trading expedition to America, with his brothers, in a small merchant ship, laden with dried fruits and wines from the Levant. After they had made an advantageous sale of their articles of traffic, it was decided among the family of brothers, that the eldest of the four,

"John Neoptolemus," should remain in New Orleans, set up a small shop, which the family were to keep supplied with fruits and wines, etc., while the other three brothers were to return home for a fresh cargo. John Neoptolemus was a shrewd trader. He spoke several tongues fluently, was clever and insinuating. He prospered, made some money for his brothers, and a great deal for himself. In course of time he extended his business, built a fine warehouse, and became famous as a dealer in wines. He speculated in cotton, in sugar, in stocks, in everything; was fortunate, and grew to be a millionnaire. At more than middle age he married the pretty Miss Canonge, who died at the birth of Natika.

Natika was brought up chiefly by her aunt, Mrs. Burthe, who loved the little girl almost as much as she did her only son, Victor, who was two years younger than Natika. All three daughters of Docteur Canonge, Mrs. Jacquimin, Mrs. Burthe and Mrs. Bolling, seemed to be of delicate constitution, for they died off one after another, leaving the already widowed old docteur very lonely in the world. He was very glad to get control of his grandson, Mark Bolling, at the time of his son-in-law Bolling's second marriage with Mrs. Coolidge. Mark was a very precious treasure to the old man. He had not seen very much of his other two grandchildren, though they were sent occasionally to visit him by their respective parents and guardians.

Natika was a delicate child, partly perhaps from being deprived of her mother's care at such an early age and also from over-indulgence in all her capricious tastes and wilful imprudences from the time that she was conscious of possessing a will of her own. Her aunt Burthe never said her nay, and her father was too much absorbed in his business to give much time to the bringing up of his only child. He saw Natika occasionally, either in his own home, where she was intrusted to the care of well-paid but careless servants, or at her aunt Burthe's, where she spent most of her time. He saw that she was exceedingly pretty and graceful, intelligent and bright, and he was satisfied.

Natika was treated like a little queen in her aunt's house; and Victor was taught, from his earliest years, to submit to her imperiousness, and to look upon her as a creature quite superior to ordinary human beings. Natika was very much quicker in intellect than Victor. She had all the readiness and suppleness which the long, back-stretching generations of culture give to the pure Greek mind. She was as versatile in her talents as Alcibiades himself, and might have held her own with an Aspasia, or a Deidamia, the gifted friend of Socrates; and with this Greek subtlety of nature was combined the light, mercurial " chauvinisme " of her mother's French blood.

Natika was true for the moment; but possession

of any coveted pleasure brought with it immediate satiety and weariness. Nothing satisfied her; she found excitement in the pursuit, but never in the attainment of her wishes. She was the true daughter of those Athenians who, as St. Paul says, "were never weary to hear or to tell of some new thing," and yet this very versatility and changefulness gave a piquancy and attraction to Natika which also made of her a Cleopatra, whom age could not wither nor custom stale in her infinite variety. The truth of her momentary impulses made them strangely fascinating, while her caprices tortured, and her total lack of power of devotion and self-abnegation, qualities which seem to be essentially womanly, made Natika a perpetual disappointment and cause of anguish to all who really loved her. She was so unstable, and so fond of power, that sometimes she seemed to be utterly merciless and cold, when she was only weary. Intellectual pleasures would have given her some sort of real satisfaction; but Natika, while she would read all day sometimes, and listen with clear understanding to any intellectual conversation, had never the steadiness of purpose to *study* anything. What she knew, she picked up without trouble. She *would not* be troubled about anything! *"It did not pay,"* she said.

Any nouveauté amused her for a day; then it wearied her; then she hated it. She had no conception of duty, or of self-sacrifice. There were no possibilities of any heroism in her. She was born a Sybarite; but an intellectual one, for there was no coarseness in Natika. Such as she was, she was passionately followed and adored by higher and better natures than hers ever could become. But high and heroic deeds, even, would have wearied Natika. She did not like the demands such natures made upon her—demands that it was utterly impossible for her nature to meet satisfactorily. It was not in her to be constant and to love nobly. Why should more be demanded of any organization than it is capable of?

To Panola, Natika felt an instinctive dislike. She did not like her beauty. She did not like her wonderful violin-playing. She did not like the singleness and utter simplicity of manner, or the semi-stoical nature, or the self-control and reticence which were Panola's inheritance from her long generations of warrior ancestors. Natika felt instinctively the dawning possibilities of a heroism and magnanimity in Panola that she herself was incapable of; and she did not like her. Neither did she like the expression of Mark Bolling's face, when he spoke of Panola; nor Victor's loudly proclaimed admiration of her beauty; though he confessed Panola had "no *style*" whatever.

Natika's father had been dead for several years, and she was left utterly unfettered by home-ties of any sort at her majority. She had put her business affairs into the hands of responsible guardians, and she had gone to Europe, where she lived the half-Bedouin life of wandering Americans, changing her residence from city to city as it suited her whim. She had still relatives living in Greece, and one uncle survived, who was a large banker in Constantinople; and she had a cousin in trade in Cairo, Egypt. She renewed her intercourse by letter with these nearly forgotten relatives, and she frequently threatened Victor with running away from the "wearisome civilization of Europe," to take refuge in the more lax conventionalisms of the East. The life of a wandering tourist was too objectless to satisfy Natika. She liked novelty; but she had no sentimentality with any past, no respect for tradition in any form, no reverence for anybody or anything, and she hated the trouble of sight-seeing. She liked *people* and *society*. She had been compelled to visit America and her native State on account of some business arrangements; and while she was in Louisiana, she thought she might as well pay her grandfather Canonge a visit. So she had come. And Victor, who had followed her from Europe to New Orleans, followed her also to their grandfather's. The gentle-hearted old man was overcome with joy at seeing them. His expressions of delight and gratitude really awoke some response of affection in the hearts of his selfish grandchildren, Victor and Natika.

Mark attracted them also.   Natika was very glad she *had* come to visit her grandfather, and she made herself fascinating and charming to her grandfather and to her cousins.   Her feelings to Mark she scarcely understood herself.   She felt the nearest approach to love, pure and unselfish, towards Mark, that she ever was conscious of experiencing in all her life.   But she knew that any passion for Mark was a foolish expenditure of sentiment.   He could never marry, as he was; and if he ever did, Natika feared that it would not be her that he would ask to share his lot.   She believed it might be Panola! She was wiser than Panola, and could read all the signs of passion, even when repressed by Mark's resolute will, and she did not like Panola any the better for that.

CHAPTER VI.

CHEROKEE JOE SUSPECTS.

MARK was sitting in his usual place by his study table, busily reading a medical work which the servant, by his direction, had brought to him out of his grandfather's fine library.   Old Docteur Canonge had a passion for books, was a great reader himself, and a good writer in his own language. He had written much for medical works and reviews, and he was also a good *bookbinder*. His father, an emigré of distinction from the troublous times in France, had had his son carefully instructed in this trade, while he gave him opportunities of improvement in his professional studies. He said : " It was very well to be Monsieur the Marquis de Canonge ; but the Docteur Canonge and the *bookbinder* Canonge could make bread for himself when the Marquis could not." So the old docteur had kept up for amusement the trade his father had taught him in prudent care for the future. His library was therefore not only beautiful in contents, but it was likewise beautiful in exterior ; for he had rebound every volume nearly with his own careful hands, and his books, next to Mark, were the pride of his life.

Mark sat reading for some hours, undisturbed by voice or noise. There was no sound except the pleasant sighing of the wind in the great tree-tops, and the singing of the innumerable birds with which the country abounds. High above all and through all was heard the gush of irrepressible joy which flows in a liquid melody (almost perpetually, it seems) from the throats of the mocking-birds. Docteur Canonge petted the birds ; he never allowed them to be disturbed, and they were not timid in his grounds, where a shot was never fired, out of con-

sideration for them. So it was a sort of bird paradise, where they loved and quarrelled and fought
and sung all day and all night long. The sound
of cattle bells, the lowing of cows, the bleating of
sheep, and all the lovely country tones, came softened
from the distant pastures and farm-yards; and occasionally the merry laugh of a good-humored
negro as he wended his way past the house, in ex-
changing homely compliments with Lizbette, would
reach Mark's ear as he sat reading in his lonely
chamber.

The day was far advanced into the afternoon
when Victor came in, flushed from riding. He
flung his hat and whip on one chair, and himself on
another. Mark good-humoredly looked up from
his book; he was fond of Victor.

"Had a pleasant ride, Victor?" he asked.

"Very pleasant, indeed. I went over to see
Miss Flanoy and the Duplessis, '*all zie familles Duplessis,*'" said Victor, laughingly imitating his grandfather. "What merry people they are! None but
French people could live that way—all on one
place, in those little, separate cottages clustered
around Monsieur Duplessis père's house! Just like
the old Trojans—king Priam and his family! They
are so harmonious and perfectly content. Americans or English would quarrel. It is because the
French are so courteous to each other in their daily
life. An American or Englishman thinks it not

worth while to be so polite, or to say amiable things to members of his own family. He is half ashamed of his best sentiments, and only parades his disagreeable ones ; while a Frenchman expresses his emotions, and is not ashamed to love or be polite every day, 'as well as on holy days.' "

"I believe there is a good deal of truth in what you say, but it is partly because the Englishman or American is afraid of being dishonest or false, and of exaggeration in his sentiments. But perhaps it is the better fault, if I may say so, to err in excess of appearance of amiability, even if it be not entirely sincere. I believe with Bain, in his 'Psychology,' that the cultivation of our moral or any other mode or quality of thought or character, is vitally important, and if we keep a resolute *habit* of cheerfulness and of amiability, it will gradually become strong and confirmed in us to a real involuntary quality of mind or manner."

"So, then, you believe conscience is not innate, but an educated proclivity of the rational soul, Mark?" said Victor, sententiously, laughing with his eyes.

"Yes. While I think that one receives from the circumstances of birth a proclivity to understand right or wrong, the true way to acquire moral sense is to do the thing that is right," replied Mark, earnestly.

"Then if one does habitually wrong, one blunts

his conscience until at last he won't have any," persisted Victor.

"Pretty much so, I think. We generally end in *being* what we only *seem* at first."

"Rather hard lines on a poor fellow like me, Mark," said Victor, laughing. "I fear I am deteriorating dreadfully and will soon be worse off than Peter Schlemil was without his shadow, if I lose all my *conscience!* I don't half like the prospect."

"Every evil action you do, Victor, blunts your moral sense and degrades you as an 'intelligent,' as Kant calls it," insisted Mark.

"Confound it, don't preach, Mark," said Victor, springing up. "You make a fellow feel bad. Nobody wishes to be degraded in his humanity because he gives way a little to youthful folly now and then."

"It is not I—it is the Nemesis of fixed laws of sequence that pronounces the doom, Victor," said Mark. "You know yourself that the *muscles and nerves* you use the most are the strongest. It is so in mental and moral life."

"Ah, bah!" said Victor. "Let me tell you about my ride, and the fair Panola. It is surprising what a beauty that little pale white creature has developed into. I had quite an eventful ride. Just as I came in sight of the place I met Cherokee Joe lounging along the road, his blanket strapped around him, and his rifle on his shoulder, with a

6

couple of mangy curs at his heels. He was going out to shoot on the prairie. I stopped to ask him about the shooting. He says there are plenty of blue and green winged teal, and snipe too, frequenting on what he calls 'the ponds,' scattered about in this interminable prairie. How long *is* this prairie land? Where does it end? Has it a beginning? I am inclined to doubt if it has. It is prairie, prairie, everywhere, as far as I can see, with those little spots of woods that fringe the aforesaid 'ponds' in the low places, which are nothing but the drainage places of this prairie."

"The prairie extends over two hundred miles," said Mark, "back to the Sabine river, the division line between Louisiana and Texas. It begins in the lowlands on the Mississippi river. Then comes the 'Cotes Geleés,' which are rather more undulating than the lowlands; then the flat rolling prairie of the Attakapas region—a real sea of grass, green and billowy, not of sage brushes, like the northern and western prairies, and there are an immense number of those 'ponds,' as you call them, scattered all through it; famous spots for ducks and snipe, I know."

"Joe said," continued Victor, "that there were plenty of partridges, too, on the prairie. I shall go out soon and try my luck at them. What a queer fellow that Joe is, Mark! A real Indian. He seems much more adapted to the outward gear of the Indian as he was to-day, than when he accompanies the fair Panola as an escort in modern toggery. An Indian should never give up his blanket. He wears that or dressed skins with grace. He looks worse without it than a Roman senator without his toga. The blanket belongs to the Indian, and the variegated *head handkerchief* to the African, and the turban to the Orientals! They never look well without these adjuncts. I may as well smoke while we talk," and Victor drew out his cigar case, selected a cigar for Mark and one for himself, took out a small silver match-box, lighted his cigar, then offered it to Mark to light his from.

These important operations were performed in silence and solemnity. Then after a few preparatory puffs from both, Victor began again. "Well, as I was saying, I met Joe swinging himself in that Indian trot, putting one foot straight before the other, and glancing, in that quick, suspicious, restless way they all have of looking, on every side of him. By the way, Mark, that is the only thing that spoils Panola. She even has retained that restless, rapid glancing of the eyes, though in her it reminds one of the quick, bright eyes of the water-fowl, like the kingfisher. Joe, confound his ugly phiz, looks more like an old, suspicious, gaunt wolf. Well, Joe and I had quite a long talk. At least I talked and Joe said 'ugh' with a wonderful variety of inflections in his grunts. It is almost a vocabulary in itself, the 'ugh' of an Indian. I asked Joe if Miss Panola was at home.

"'Panola stay home to-day,' said the unceremonious Indian, ignoring the title of 'Miss' entirely. 'Joe go hunt. Panola stay with mother, with Chicora.'"

"Yes. That's Mrs. Flanoy's Indian name," put in Mark, taking his cigar out of his lips to give vent to a puff of smoke.

"What does it mean? These are delicious Havanas, I declare! See how long the ash holds on to the end of the cigar. We never get such in Europe."

"I really believe (puff) that I prefer (puff) a Powhatan pipe with good perrique," replied Mark, with intervals of smoke between his words. "It means (puff) 'Mocking Bird,' or, as it is in full Cherokee, 'Chicora Chee-squah-con-nau-gee-tah'— 'The bird that sing the best.'—Chicora was famous for her beauty and singularly sweet voice—a quality of voice often found in Indian women."

"Well, this 'mocking-bird' that I saw to-day was quite different from her sisters in the tree branches about her house. Her singing and dancing is all done for. She is rather a dusky old bird now."

"Chicora! Why, I think her still beautiful. What a fellow you are, Victor," said Mark, half-smiling, in spite of himself. "You ought to feel sympathy for that poor afflicted woman. Anybody else would."

"So I am, dreadfully sorry. Panola is so very pretty. Well, Joe said Panola would stay with Chicora to-day. 'Chicora velly bad,' said Joe, shaking his wild Indian locks solemnly, and regarding me with a curious, half-questioning look out of his contracted eyes. His pupils gleamed out like a black lynx's. Indians are not evolved yet wholly out of fierce beasts into perfect humanity. 'Chicora not move hands now any more,' and will you believe it, Mark, the fellow's keen eyes actually twinkled through tears that he would not let fall.

"'What do you mean, Joe?' I asked, beginning to feel somewhat alarmed about going to the house. 'Is Mrs. Flanoy ill? Are you afraid she is going to die?'

"'No, Chicora not die to-day—not yet—she die bime-by. Hands stiff now. Soon head get stiff, then heart get stiff, and Chicora die. Joe sorry, Joe much sorry for Chicora. Satana be velly sorry. He like Chicora heap—plenty much. Tribe be sorry; all Cherokees cry; plenty, heap! Ugh!'

"'What's the matter with Mrs. Flanoy, Joe?'

"'Joe not know. Canonge he not know. Nobody know. Nana say "conjure." You know Nana, Victor Burthe.'

"'No, Joe, I have not that honor. Who is Nana?'

"'Nana ole nigger 'ooman, hundred year ole—go

so!' And Joe bent himself down nearly double, and crept feebly forward, imitating the old crone. He has talent, has Joe. Then he straightened himself upright, and spat upon the earth, in token of his intense disgust, and said 'ugh,' scornfully. How Indians do hate negroes, Mark."

"Yes! Mrs. Flanoy will only use white servants about her person."

"Well! This primitive gentleman—for Joe has all the characteristics of a gentleman, you know: he hates work, and loves sport and idleness—"

"And whiskey," put in Mark.

"Yes, and whiskey, as much as any Scotch or Irish gentleman of high degree. This noble red man gave me to understand that Nana was a witch; that she ought to be killed, but there was no way to scalp her, as she hadn't a hair on her old bald head; and that it would be of no use to kill her, for she could change herself into anything she chose—a cat, or dog, or even into a snake, and then reassume her human form—that she was much petted, and noticed by 'Madame Bolling.'

"'You know Madame Bolling?' asked Joe, looking queerly up into my face, as I sat above him on my horse.

"I told him 'I had that felicity.' 'Ugh!' said Joe, puzzled by the word *felicity*. 'Ugh! you *likee* Madame Bolling velly much, Victor Burthe?'

"I told him I was passionately devoted to her in her *absence*.

"Joe looked at me. 'Ugh,' he said. He did not quite comprehend my meaning. Then he put his hand into his pocket, and pulled out a very dirty purse made of deer-skin. He opened it, took out a couple of papers. One had a fine white powder in it. Joe handed it up to me.

"'What that?' he asked. 'You know, Victor Burthe?'

"I smelled the paper, looked at the powder, took the least particle possible of it on my finger tip, and touched my tongue with it, being very careful to spit it out, you may be sure."

"That was very foolish, Victor. It might have been arsenic or morphine," interrupted Mark.

"Well, the Indian wanted to know, and how the d——l was I to tell him unless I examined?" said Victor, lightly. "However my rashness caused no harm, for it was only tartar emetic, and I told Joe it was that.

"'You makee him lemonade?' asked the Indian. I suppose he had heard of *cream of tartar* lemonade.

"'Good Lord, no,' I said, '*make lemonade!* Why it would kill you; make you sick; it is medicine.' Then I explained to Joe how it was used. Joe listened attentively, his face bent down over the paper of powder.

"'Canonge, he give it?' asked Joe.

"I said I supposed he did often give it.

"'Ugh,' said Joe, and he put the paper, carefully wrapped up, back into his old dirty purse, as if it was precious.

"'You had better throw it away, Joe,' I said.

"'No, Joe not throw away. Joe take to Satana, bime-by. Ugh.'

"I wonder what the chief will do with such a present? Then Joe opened another little paper which had some peas in it.

"'What that?' said the foolish Indian, pouring the peas into my hand.

"'That? Why those are *peas*.'

"'What good for? Medicine too?'

"'No. Good to eat, you silly fellow, like all other peas.'

"'Ugh! You likee eat peas? Joe give you some.' And he took a small parcel of them, and gave them to me. 'Eatee some, Victor Burthe!'

"'No, I thank you, Joe. When I eat peas I like them cooked, not raw.'

"'Ugh!' Joe folded up his peas in his piece of paper and put *them* into his purse. 'Joe take to Satana,' said Joe, thoughtfully. 'Ugh! got any whiskey, Victor Burthe?'

"I told him I had not, but I gave him a couple of cigars and a half dollar to buy whiskey, and Joe shouldered his gun, and with a parting 'ugh' he trotted off, and I galloped on.

"Well, I had already passed the little place called

the Pavilion, where Mrs. Bolling lives now; you know it is just outside the Flanoy place, not more than a stone's throw from the gates; you remember the yard runs down to the road of this aforesaid Pavilion. What a small affair it is in the way of a house!"

"It has four rooms in it," said Mark, "and is built, like all the other houses in this county, of one story. We can't build high, you know, on account of the strong winds which blow over this prairie country, coming from the Gulf of Mexico; they would blow down lofty houses."

"Well, it looks very modest, but is snug enough, I dare say, and large enough too, for Madame Bolling's requirements. It is rather picturesque, with the luxuriant vines trained on wires all around the verandah. I had already got past, when I was hailed by Antony Coolidge, who was standing at the gate, with his arms folded on the top of it, like 'Yankee Doodle dandy.'"

> "'Who swung upon the gates,
> And licked 'lasses candy,'"

laughed Mark.

"Yes, exactly, barring the candy. Unfortunately for the rhyme, on this occasion Yankee Doodle was smoking a cigarette. He invited me to stop, and as I had no good reason for declining his invitation, and wasn't pressed for time, I concluded I would get off my horse for a minute. I don't dislike

Antony, at least comparatively speaking: he is less disagreeable to me than his mamma, that 'veuve charmante,' as our respected and beloved progenitor calls her. The truth was I wanted to see the inside of 'the shebang.'"

"For goodness sake, Victor, don't use so much slang. Why can't you talk respectably decent English, or French, if you like?" said Mark, smiling.

"Because I am talking *American* and about *American* people; very truly and positively *American* people. Aboriginal *Americans*, like the fair Panola and the old Mocking Bird," replied the incorrigible Victor. "I shall tell my story in my own style, Mark, if you choose to listen, and, unlike the amiable Scherazade, I detest interruptions, especially when they are criticisms."

"On with you then, you incorrigible fellow," said Mark, good-humoredly. "You accepted Antony's invitation and went into the—"

"Shebang," interposed Victor. "It was really beautiful in the verandah; it was literally curtained in with an enormous bean vine, a lineal descendant of Jack's bean-stalk."

"It is a cork-screw bean. They do grow to a most extraordinary size here," interrupted Mark.

"This one fellow twisted himself all around the verandah, and was hanging thick with the greatest profusion of purple and yellow flowers, and the perfume was nearly overpowering, it was so strong.

Antony took me inside. It is very nice inside the house too. We found that Madame Mère was in the garden. So we went out there. The house was filled with pets—dogs and cats and canary birds."

"The African nature delights in pets," observed Mark, thoughtfully.

"Precisely! oh, supreme wonder among psychologists," said Victor, waving his cigar towards Mark. "There was also a green parrot who swore astonishingly in French. Does your stepmother indulge in that luxury also, Mark?"

"Pshaw," said Mark, not deigning to resent the impertinent inquiry.

"Ah," said Victor, giving a long puff, and then knocking the ash from the end of his cigar, where it had been tenaciously accumulating. "If she *don't*, *where* did *the parrot learn?* However, we got into the garden, a very pretty little garden back of the house, and there we found your highly revered stepmother in a house dress, with a broad straw flat tied down over her head; and quite handsome she looked, and unusually wicked was the glance of her strange eyes. I wish they had more gradation in the color of the pupil: the dead black on the dead white of the ball gives a reptilish expression to that woman that all her splendor of color can't overcome. I believe, Mark, in transmigration of life upwards, am half a Darwinian, and I am convinced, Mark, that your adorable stepmother came up into

humanity through the snakes; she was once either
a cobra di capella or a flat-headed viper."

"Oh, Victor! Victor!"

"Truth, Mark! I must speak truth to you,
even though the sky should fall. 'I can't tell a lie,
father,' as the father of his country did *never* say.
Well, the buxom dame was all smiles and welcome.
She was superintending the work of a negro man,
who was spading some ground in which she was
about to plant some seeds. Bending over one of
the drills already laid out was the old negress
Nana. I recognized her from Joe's personation.
If she is not 'a hundred,' as he said, she must be
pretty near it. I never saw such an old toothless
hag in my life, so wrinkled; you know, negroes
don't wrinkle like other people. They are *very* old
when the skin crumples up. This old creature hadn't
a hundredth part of an inch smooth on her face. She
would have been an admirable study for a modern
Andrew Denner; you know what a devotion he
had for painting wrinkles! She looked like a min-
iature rhinoceros, with her crumpled skin; and she
had got to be so old, she was a sort of ashen-black-
gray in hue; all the humanity had burnt out of her,
Mark, ages ago! I think she probably lived in the
period of Nineveh! She looked every day of it!
Do you know, Mark—it is a fact, I have been
assured so upon excellent authority—that people
live so long, sometimes, that the human soul dies

out, and then they exist only from animal vital forces. If Nana ever had a soul, which I doubt, holding with you and Herbert Spencer, and Spinoza, *et als.*, that the soul or mind is only a development, a gradual building up from the experiences of ourselves and others, the concentrated sum of the collected knowledge of past generations, plus ourselves—"

"In that case Nana should have had a pretty large soul," interpolated Mark, gravely, with his eyes twinkling.

"I have already told you she had burnt up her soul," replied Victor, seriously; "that's in accordance with your deterioration theory, you know! She has been such a wicked old wretch that she has acquired a habit of wickedness. The logic is inexpugnable! I believe that Nana, according to my theory of transmigration, was once a hyena,

> ' Where Afric's golden fountains
> Roll o'er her sunny plains.' "

> ' ' Where Afric's *sunny* fountains
> Roll o'er her *golden* plains,' "

suggested Mark. "You never quote correctly, Victor."

Victor shook his fist menacingly at Mark. "Criticisms are tabooed," said Victor. "This everlasting flower, of Africa's Hesperidean garden, whom Death and Time have forgotten, was engaged

in sticking small holes in the ground with the end
of a pointed reed. She did it *venomously*, Mark,
as if she was sticking the sharp point into the heart
of an enemy; and when I bent over to see what she
was planting, behold! they were the identical peas,
or the same sort at least, that Cherokee Joe had
shown to me a half-hour previously. I understood
at once the foolish fellow's superstition about the
innocent peas. He saw old Nana planting them,
and he believed them to be uncanny."

"Probably," said Mark.

"Madame Bolling saw my notice of old Nana's
work: 'Are you fond of flowers, Mr. Burthe?' she
said; '*I* am passionately so, especially of strong-
scented ones! Don't you like the sweet pea? It is
a favorite of mine. Let me make a bouquet for you
to give to my niece, Panola, as you say you will
ride in that direction presently.'

"So saying, she gathered me a bouquet; very gay
it was, and the strongest-smelling that ever I had;
then, as I declined her invitation to remain to
luncheon, I took the bouquet and bade her good
day. As soon as I got out of sight of Antony, I
stuck the end of my whip into the flowers, and
hoisted them up on top of a small thorn tree, and
left them to waste their sweetness there. I would
not have transported those flowers to Panola for
five thousand dollars. I know they were 'conjuring
flowers,' for old Nana planted them and Mrs. Bol-

ling gathered them; and she has an 'evil eye,' you know, Mark; I do think so."

"Pish!" ejaculated Mark; "what folly!"

"Well, after all these delays, I at last reached the gates of the enchanted castle—Mrs. Flanoy's large, wide-spreading, hospitable mansion, of which Lizbette says, 'Every room opens charmingly on the gallery, and it has twenty rooms.' I think it covers an acre and a half of ground, on a moderate calculation. It is quite handsome, and altogether civilized and Christian-like, not at all on the wigwam order of architecture, as I had half expected it to be. Indeed the salon was really French in its fittings-up, but I am not upholsterer enough to describe it, *secundum artem*. A neat, well-dressed, *white* footman received my card, and conducted me through the wide, cool hall into a side-gallery, and at length into a pretty salon, in which I found Mademoiselle Panola, who came forward to greet me. Then she led me up to a large lounge, on which lay a figure that might have been carved out of stone, so motionless was it. A rose-colored, silk quilt, filled with eider-down, lay spread over it up to the throat, and above the quilt, looking as if it was disconnected with any body, visible or invisible, lay a head. Good Lord! what a head! All the fire, force, vitality and strength of a whole human life was concentrated into that face; the whole body was dead but that; the eyes, large, dark and sad, but

with a preternatural lustre, showed a tremendous
will, a concentration of the essence of an immense
physical nature. I shall never forget those eyes and
that face! The features are not unlike Panola's:
the same firm, delicate outline; the slightly aquiline
nose; the mouth, originally sweet and haughty, like
Panola's, now compressed into thinness by intense
strain of will. It was the incarnation of will—
defiant will—and yet with a queer, sad beauty. The
eyes looked up into mine with an eager, wistful,
hungry gaze, and with such a magnetic power that
it seemed to me I felt my soul swaying under
the magic of the glance! Such passion, such
self-mastery, such pride! God! it was terrible!
I stood dumb before her; when, at last, the lips
moved, and a voice with the sound of music itself
said: 'You are welcome, Mr. Burthe!' Twenty
years ago, when that woman was young, Mark, few
men's hearts would not have yielded to the magic
of that voice and that face. Her complexion is not
white or satiny, like Panola's, but it is a rich,
whitish pink with a bronze glow through it; and
her cheeks and lips, perhaps from disease, near the
red of the pomegranate flower. But her eyes! they
are the wonder! Oh! that splendid, noble, impris-
oned, womanly soul! God! Mark! you don't
know how I longed to help that woman! She lay
there as if under the spell of some enchantment,
with none to help her. I spoke lightly of her,

Mark, when we began to talk, but you see I do not feel lightly. I can comprehend Joe's devotion, and the deep love of all around her—even of Satana, the chief! *One could adore her!* She seemed to like me.

"I stayed fully an hour there, talking to her and to Panola; and I took lunch there. Panola played wonderful things on her Straduarius, and I sung a good deal; Mrs. Flanoy asked me, and I was very glad to do it. I don't know when I should have got away, but one of the footmen came in with a note on a silver tray, which he presented ceremoniously to Panola.

"'It is for you, mamma,' said Panola.

"It was addressed to Mrs. Maria Josepha Flanoy, so you see she is not the 'Mocking-bird' to everybody."

"No," said Mark; "she has been christened Maria Josepha."

"Well, then, I rode home as fast as I could. As I passed the thorn tree, I saw that a very curious crow had picked my evil bouquet off the branch, and having it now on the ground, was conveniently tearing it into fragments with his beak and claws. He gave an ominous caw as I approached, and flew away like a bad, black spirit; and you now behold me here. Here endeth the narration of Victor, the son of Victor, the son of Philippe, the son of—"

"Spare the genealogy!" cried Mark, holding

7

up his hands in entreaty, as Victor paused to take breath. Victor replied by singing exquisitely:

> "There be none of beauty's daughters
> With a face like thee;
> And like music on the waters
> Is thy voice to me."

Whilst singing, he rose and walked out of the room, saying he would go look for Natika.

"She's gone out to drive with grandfather," called out Mark after him, as he disappeared through the doorway.

In a few moments the door opened, and Victor put in his head again.

"Oh, I forgot to tell you that, as I returned, I made a detour through the village to get our mail matter, and as I came back, who should I see in the midst of the highway, surrounded by a group of laughing children and idle men, but Cherokee Joe; who had spent my half dollar in getting gloriously drunk. There the poor fellow was in high glee, singing a wild Indian song, boastful of his triumphs in love and war, I suppose, from the pantomime with which he accompanied it. He danced the war-dance, hopping slowly and solemnly, first on one leg and then on the other, round and round in a circle; then stopping suddenly, he gave a swift run forward, scattering the children right and left as he dashed through them; seizing his hatchet, which

was swinging by a leather thong to his girdle, he
brandished it fiercely; putting one hand to his
mouth, he gave utterance to a tremendous war-
whoop, and threw the hatchet as he sprang forward,
with immense force.   It flew past my head, and
struck a tree at which he seemed to have aimed it.
I should not liked to have been the *tree!*   Then he
caught a long blow-gun out of the hands of one of
the little children, who had been playing with it—
some one had taken his own rifle away from him,
for fear of mischief, I suppose.   He seized the blow-
gun, and lifting it to his mouth, the arrow whizzed
past me, and struck into the tree just above the
hatchet.   You never saw truer shots.   Then he
looked around for admiration and applause, delighted at the children's notice and laughter, which
he esteemed to be complimentary.   Catching sight
of me, his mood seemed to change to a softer one,
or perhaps the maudlin stage was coming on.   So,
singing some Indian words, in which I distinguished
the sounds of Chicora and Panola, he sat himself
down on a bank by the roadside under the shade of
the hedge, and began to weep, swaying his body to
and fro, in sort of cadenced lament; occasionally
giving utterance to a prolonged howl that was
unearthly.   Then he grew stupid; lying down
on the grass, he fell asleep, and there I left
him."

"He is very strong," said Mark.   "I have seen

him often bend a bar of very thick iron in his hands, as if it were only wire."

"Well, a nap in the open air will refresh him. Poor wretch! one can scarcely believe him to be of the same race as Panola and that grand Chicora."

"The blood of the Netherlander has something to do with Panola," said Mark. "Chicora is only a half-breed."

"If there are any more like Chicora, in her tribe," said Victor, "it would be worth while mounting hunting-shirts and moccasins, and living in a wigwam, to see such a woman as she must have been in her full youth and health. Now, senhor, truly, adios!" said the volatile Victor.

"Vaya con Dios," responded Mark, gayly.

CHAPTER VII.

MUCH-MARRIED LIZBETTE.

DOCTEUR CANONGE stood in the library, stirring slowly with his spoon the cup of smoking-hot coffee which Lizbette had sent to him. He had been up nearly all the night previous with a poor sick neighbor, and he looked rather paler and thinner and more cadaverous than usual, though his smile was as sweet as the sunshine itself, which was pouring in a flood of golden light through the open window near which the gentle old man was standing, talking to Mark and Victor. Natika came in. "Grandpapa," she exclaimed, "I want you to drive with me to see Mrs. Flanoy this morning; can't you?"

Docteur Canonge smiled. "I haf leetle doubt żat I *will*, Natika, if you so desire. I did tink of finishing my article on comparative mythologie zis morning for zie Academie Française; but zat can wait. I shall also be ver' glad to consulte Chicora about zie Cherokee version of zie myth zat I now am attempting to explain."

"And what is that, grandpapa?" said Natika.

"It is zie pretty leetle story of Bo-peep and her sheep zat she did lose."

"And how do you explain that, grandpapa?"

"I have traced zis leetle myth through many of zie derivative languages from zie Aryan, among all zie people of zat blood and race; and I have conclude zat zis leetle myth represent zie dawn as usual wiz her clouds, which were often called 'sheep.'"

"Yes," interrupted Victor, "Shelley speaks of them—the clouds 'shepherded by the wind.'"

"Yes. I am much obliged, Victor, for zie suggestion of zose lines of Shelley."

"But what about the 'tails' of Bo-peep's sheep?" asked Natika, gayly. "Clouds have none."

"Yes, they have," interposed Mark. "Sailors call those sweeping, streaky clouds, 'mares' tails.'"

"Yes," said Docteur Canonge, nodding his head approvingly.

"But," remonstrated Natika, "those are rain clouds, not dawn clouds; or at any rate they are *foretellers* of rain."

Docteur Canonge's face fell.

"But," suggested Mark, "it is all one. It may be meant that Bo-peep's dawn was not a clear one."

Docteur Canonge looked brighter.

"I think," said Victor, "the myth meant the sun and stars, especially comets, which have tails."

"But they don't lose them," said Natika.

"No, but they may be obscured," observed Mark, "for a time; that would accord with the story as it is told. They are seemingly dissipated for a time."

"Zie Ingins say zat it was not sheep, but a herd of buffaloes, zat zie leetle Bo-peep was guarding, an' zat zie buffaloes or bisons did make zie stampede an' shake zie earth till it was great earthquake, and zey did lose zeir tails."

"Shook 'em off, I suppose," said Victor, laughingly.

"About zat I am not certain," replied Docteur Canonge, gravely. "I will ask Chicora."

Mark smiled and shook his head at Victor, who was laughing. Mark was very tender of his grandfather's crotchets.

"But, as regards zose comets' tails—ah, yes," said the old docteur, pursing his lips thoughtfully as he spoke, "and also M. Guillemin says, in his work upon comets, zat zese wandering stars are perpetually robbed of zeir gaseous particles, zeir nebulous tails, as zey do pass amongst zie constellations. Yet I do prefer zie myth of zie dawn clouds for leetle Bo-peep. Still I shall consider zie tails of zie comets, Victor. It is a good suggestion and worthy of remark, my dear."

Victor looked ashamed.

"Grandpapa, you are so good," he said, and he rose and put his arm about the old man's neck.

Docteur Canonge embraced him tenderly.

During the conversation Docteur Canonge's coffee had got to be cool enough for quaffing. So he drained it to the bottom of the cup; café noir it really was, strong as any Arab of the sacred tribe of the Wahabtees ever distilled for his own holy lips.

Lizbette excelled in coffee and in all the real Southern dishes. She made both the gumbos, as well as the famous bisque, to perfection. It takes exactly one hundred and fifty crawfish to make a good dish of bisque. Lizbette understood how to divide them—so many for stuffed heads, so many for stuffing, so many for beating up into powder, so many for the basis of the soup. There are some things in this world that only a Creole cook can do.

One is to make bisque. Then Lizbette knew all about terrapin, all about corn-bread, and rice waffles, and hominy, and capons, and "pain perdu." She knew how to make fig conserves, and watermelon citron, and cocoanut cakes, and banana fritters, the very coolest of ices and sherbets, and drinks of fruit juices—that made from the yellow fruit of the passion vine up to the syrup of orange blossoms, whose "bouquet" was as exquisite as its "gout."

In 'short, Lizbette was perfection itself, in the kitchen, over the pots and pans. But, out of it, she would occasionally get on a "rampage," especially when she got "*na that fou, but just a drappie in her e'e;*" which sometimes happens in a better regulated household than Docteur Canonge's. In truth, this household was somewhat irregular and even Bohemian in its arrangements. There were no especial hours for anything, except dinner. Docteur Canonge could never be counted on for any meal, for sleep, or for any regularity of living, because he was subject to constant calls in his profession, and ate and slept and came home when he could. But Lizbette had always something hot and good ready for him, at any hour of the day or night; especially did the coffee dripper simmer and moan away all the time beside the kitchen fire, on its own particular little charcoal furnace.

Coffee was the one necessity of life for Docteur Canonge and his household. Tea he disdained, and they all thought themselves *very* ill when they were condemned " to tea and toast." The contortions of visage with which the beverage would be swallowed would be inconceivable to any Englishman. But the fact was, Lizbette did not make good tea. Either she steeped it in middling cool water, or she boiled it, or stewed it, or did something to it which drew out all its bitterness and evaporated all its aroma. Then, too, these ignorant people had never drunk a cup of really *good* tea, made as it is in England. So they only knew it through Lizbette's preparations. (I should advise any Englishman who travels in Louisiana, to bring with him his own portable little tea equipage, or learn to drink coffee or claret for his breakfast. The tea is generally abominable stuff.)

Tisans can be got to perfection. Tisans of balm, or orange leaves, or violets, or of the thousand plants that are used by experienced French nurses for the simple cure or prevention of native diseases. On the opposite side of the fireplace to the coffee furnace Lizbette usually had a caraffe of "Tisan" stewing for some body or other.

Lizbette was part of the family. She ruled over the other servants despotically, and whenever she got a little too much " old Bourbon " or " Jamaiky," she used to sit down and weep bitterly, and tear her hair, in memory of her "dear dead old mistus," Mrs. Canonge, who had been buried for forty years.

Then the old docteur would shrug his shoulders, give Lizbette a few drops of ammonia, and have her put in her bed, whence, after a few hours' sleep, she would emerge meek and subdued, and altogether amiable and obliging for some time.

While Natika and Victor were with their grand-papa, Mark made an effort to have a little more regularity about the household, and did succeed with lunch and dinner; but breakfast remained woefully protracted and long drawn out. Victor would come sometimes to join Mark at nine o'clock. Natika tried it once, and then ordered her chocolate at eleven. Victor fell off too in attendance. Docteur Canonge came *sometimes*, but not often. So Mark returned to his old habits of his simple, solitary breakfast at eight o'clock, leaving the others to arrange their own hours with Lizbette.

Docteur Canonge's house was really a very delightful restaurant, where each and all did exactly as they pleased. Nobody was in a hurry about anything in particular, and the servants rather liked the disjointed style of living.

Negroes have naturally no instinct of order. They sleep anywhere and at all hours, and rise often to cook and eat at the most untimely hours of the night. Victor called his grandfather's house "Liberty Hall." He said it was a good name for an American house. He liked it better than "Independence Hall." It was more characteristic. Yet,

over all this freedom there prevailed an atmosphere
of gracious courtesy and refinement which took its
rise in the heart of the old French docteur.

Lizbette had recently buried her eighth husband ;
not that she had been a widow eight times.   Only
two of her husbands had been taken away by a
"decree of Providence," as Lizbette and the coro-
ners express it.   The other six had been divorced or
abandoned by her, as she became weary of their
conjugal society, though she had been lawfully married to each of them (Lizbette was a strict Methodist
and particular about the conventionalities of religion).   But when she was weary of a husband, she
used to have a grand quarrel and separate à mensâ
et thorâ.

Lizbette's ideas of law being rather confused, she
considered that equal to a divorce anywhere ; so,
when she was attracted by another man, she duly
married him according to her ideas of law and order.
She was faithful while she lived with her husbands,
and cut them off entirely when she was fatigued
with their society.   However, she bore no malice,
and was quite friendly after the lapse of a few
months intercourse ; and the "divorced ones" used
to visit her occasionally, and she was always ready
to give them a friendly meal, or any little help in
life.   She also visited their wives on quite an intimate footing.   The principles of the free-lovers
were practically exemplified every day by Lizbette

and her people, and they never lost caste among themselves, or in their church, by these small domestic difficulties. Indeed, three of Lizbette's husbands were preachers, and stood high in the opinion of the sable brethren and sisters.

There is no doubt that the higher sentiments of constant love to one and monogamy is the last result of European civilization and of man's development in the last twenty centuries. It began first in the West among the Romans, as a matter of state policy; was incorporated into Christianity not only by the teachings of its Divine Founder but also as a matter of social civilization and statesmanship. The highest problems of civilization have been worked out through it. But it is not natural to the African. They have not yet attained to the highest sentiment of a constant love. They are a child-people, with the virtues and the vices belonging to a child-people. They have no idea of vengeance, except for the moment; neither of gratitude, except for the time. Unless the blood is mixed : then the mulatto inherits the strong passions and appetencies of one race and the astuteness and viciousness of the whites. While he is ordinarily more intellectual, he is not so good, nor so docile, nor so affectionate as a pure black; and he has more the sentiment of revenge, but no more gratitude. A child is rarely grateful. It takes all favors joyfully, but without sense of obligation, and it forgets in a moment; and so does the African.

They are a kind, impulsive people, governed by *à priori* superstitions. They may be developed out of this, but they will then be developed into another race of beings.

Lizbette, with all her deficiencies, was a very important and greatly beloved member of Docteur Canonge's family, but she was African au fond.

NOTE.—Among the Hindoos we find the most delicate and beautiful pictures of purest conjugal love. For instance, in the loves of Rama and Sita, in Sakuntala, and other earliest books, which portray the Hindoo ideal. Even the *Suttee* sprang from this elevated ideal of the oneness of conjugal lives. Perhaps it is from the Aryan that the European sentiment of constancy may be inherited; and its pure conception of conjugal unity comes from the people who imagined Sita and Sakuntala.

CHAPTER VIII.

A GERMAN NATURALIST.

"GRANDPAPA," Mark exclaimed, one morning, as the docteur was passing to and fro in the little workroom adjoining the library, where poor Mark usually could be found, seated eternally, with his books and writing materials conveniently disposed about him : "grandpapa, here is a letter you will enjoy, from Professor Römer."

"Römer! indeed, I shall much delight in dat!" responded the docteur, hastening into the library, regardless of his peculiar appearance, being clad in a long blue linen blouse over his usual attire, having his head tied up in a bright bandana handkerchief, to keep off the dust; his hands being extended outwards from his person, for they were full of paste and gum—he had been occupied in rebinding some of his treasures of old or rare books —his long, narrow, thin, French face sparkling with anticipated pleasure.

"Dat is great man! Römer! great botaniste! I like his books ver mooch. I have zem all bound in zie beautiful red lezzer. I do it myself. I like Römer!"

Victor had been reading George Sand's last romance, with his heels higher than his head, as he lay upon a sofa in the library. He put down his book and sat upright as his grandfather came running in, so full of eagerness about the letter Mark held open in his hand. Victor was not at all scientific, but he *had* heard of Römer, whose reputation was world-wide.

"Where did you meet Römer?" asked Victor, with interest.

"I met him in Berlin," said Mark. "I saw a good deal of him, and grew to be much attached to him, and we have corresponded in a desultory sort of fashion ever since. He is now in South America, and this letter has been wandering about a good deal, being first brought down one of the tributaries of the Amazon on the head of one of the Indian swimmers who transport the mail in that region of cataracts and vast trackless forests."

"I am altogedder attention," said Docteur Canonge; "read on, Mark."

"Does he write English?" asked Victor; "it does not look like English from here."

"No; he writes in German, and that's the reason it has been so long reaching me," replied Mark. "Our postmasters don't generally read German text."

"I don't understand it either, Mark; so you had better translate," proposed Victor. "I should like to hear what Römer says for himself."

Mark glanced over the letter. "Well, it is great injustice to Römer, who is really quite eloquent in his own tongue; but here goes for an off-hand translation, literal, of course."

"My Dear Mark:—You do not think that I have forgotten you, because I have not found time this present year to write to you, noble friend. I have been very busy, and in many wild regions of the earth, where correspondence was not a possibility; where there were no roads and no mail facilities, not even such as are here, of an Indian swimmer to convey a letter upon his head, down the rivers for many miles, to points of civilization. Owing to the frequent cataracts and pathless forests, there is no other good route for anything less persevering than an enthusiastic botanist, who discovers here in this untrodden wilderness a true paradise, in which, I assure you, serpents abound, although the Eves are by no means tempting. I have been wandering, since the last year, gathering abundance of finest specimens of plants for the Berlin museum. I have been extremely successful and immensely happy. I have found several new varieties of cinchona, and one *fern*, which grows only in a cavern on a certain tributary of the Amazon, a fern never known before, and which I risked my life, with joy, to obtain. It grew in a cave, into which I had to be lowered by a grass rope, on the side of a mountain much broken by rocks, about three hundred feet. The Indians who were my guides objected to my descent; but I gave them my only overcoat, well lined with sable (a present from King William, which had served me well on my travels), but I had forgotten to bring any money from the last town whence I started to make this little tour, so I had bartered away all I had with me, except my pipe, a shirt, my trowsers and this overcoat, which I now gave to be permitted to make this descent. I had no shoes, save the cowskin sewed boots of this country, and I have now an overcoat like a Tartar's, made of dressed sheepskins, so I could not make a creditable appearance with you as formerly 'Unter

den Linden,' in Berlin. I was in a little danger lest
the rocks might cut my grass rope, at the end of
which I dangled for a half hour; but at last I made
my footing safe into the mouth of the cavern, and I
found the fern. Oh, mein lieber Mark! but it was
an hour of joy. I grasped my treasure, and put it
safely into my little silver box in my bosom; then I
seized another handful—roots and all—and gave the
signal to be hoisted up, which was done quickly;
but, having to guard my precious plant, I could not
protect myself from the rocks so well, and so I received some rather sharp blows on my body, which
have rendered me somewhat stiff in the shoulders
and elbows, and forced me to rest a few days. So I am
compelled to take leisure, and I write up my letters:
this one to you, dear beloved Mark. I had a small
attack of fever of the country this year, for about
two months. It was intermittent in type, and gave
me an opportunity of testing the strength of the
different varieties of the cinchona, which I took in
infusion and also in decoction. I am, therefore, now
prepared to give experimental information in regard
to the qualities of the different plants as febrifuges.
I tried some of the coarser and weaker sorts faith-
fully for several weeks; but they did not relieve
disease so quickly as others. I can advise the government positively on this matter. I did not mind
retaining my fever somewhat longer, in order to
attain to this certain knowledge.

8

"This is a splendid country for a botanist. I do not know when I can persuade myself to leave it. I find so much that is delightful here. I have learned to live like the people here, and it does very well indeed. Sometimes I find I can go very well for several days, as the Arabs do, with the sustenance of small balls of ground coffee, which I can generally obtain in this latitude. It is very convenient, and easily portable."

"Good Lord!" ejaculated Victor, "what a diet!"

Mark smiled as he glanced up from his letter. Docteur Canonge was rubbing his hands in glee. Römer was a man after his own heart.

"Oh, but I *should* like to eat coffee wiz such a compagnon!" said the docteur; "it would be nectare of zie gods!"

"Besides," continued Mark, reading, "I have frequently much fruits and many plants which are edible and known to me, so that I fare well. Some day you will find me knocking at your gate, dear Mark, when, if ever, I can persuade myself to quit this land of interest and wonders. Make my compliments to your venerable and most admired grandfather, Monsieur le Marquis and Docteur Canonge, whom I hope some day to see, and to lay at his feet my most respectful homage. With unchanging friendship, believe me, my dear Mark,

"Yours,   "RÖMER."

"Dat is a man! a man among zouzands!" commented Docteur Canonge, clasping his paste-covered fingers together enthusiastically. "It is a friend to be proud for, my dear Mark!"

Victor ran his fingers through his soft, dark curls and looked laughingly at his grandfather.

"Yes," responded Mark, earnestly, "Römer is a magnificent fellow! I *am* proud of his friendship. Oh, how gladly I would partake in his fatigues and dangers, if it were but possible!" and Mark sighed heavily as he glanced at his faultless but helpless legs.

Docteur Canonge's face changed. He never could bear to hear Mark sigh over his helpless condition.

"I mus' go and complete zic binding of my 'Bœthius,'" he said, "while zic paste remains still soft. I zank you, dear Mark, for reading me Römer's beautiful letter."

The old docteur never forgot his graceful courtesy towards the most intimate associate; he smiled gratefully on his grandson, and disappeared into his own sanctum to his work.

He had hardly got his leather straight upon his book's back before the door opened.

"Grandpapa," cried Natika, entering hurriedly into his laboratory, "you'll have to stop your work! Here come three carriages, containing, I think, *all* the Smiths and *all* the Clarks to pay their party call!"

Docteur Canonge held up his pasty hands in despair, shrugged his shoulders, and then, with a comical grimace, said:

"Zey make attack in a phalanx! How sall we meet zis enemy?"

Natika laughed. "I don't know, grandpapa. Let's bring them all in here, where Mark and Victor can help us; and tell Lizbette to send up a tray of wine and little cakes as soon as possible, and some of her home-made orange syrup and water."

"Yes; zat will be a diversion to occupy zie army for a while," said Docteur Canonge, laughing. "And we will tell zem about Römer, and I will show zem my workshop. So, now we have arrange our plan of battle, I will go wash my hands and take off zis workman's costume!"

When Docteur Canonge returned to the salon after making a hurried toilette, he came in all the splendor of his black suit, in the buttonholes of which dangled the ribands of several scientific associations, among them the red riband of the French academy. He found "the army," as he had called it, already in line of battle. The angular Mr. Clark, the exuberant Mrs. Clark, the shy Miss Clark, occupied one sofa in a straight line; immediately at right angles sat the three Misses Smith, with their mamma flanking them, and their brother trying to look graceful, nonchalant and accustomed to the easy performance of all social duties. Natika sat facing this formidable array, talking volubly and despairingly—making enormous efforts to get some replies more than monosyllabic from her overwhelming and portentous guests. But they, the guests, had come to *be* entertained, not to entertain. So they sat up for their rights, and Natika found that even her Parisian skill failed when she had to do the "frais" of all the conversation for a party comprising six women, who had very few ideas, and who jealously kept those few sacredly within the miserly recesses of their own minds.

This séance was held in the chief salon, and Natika could have embraced her grandfather, when after making his graceful and gracious salutations, he invited the whole party to adjourn to the library. So that his poor Mark "also might have zie pleasure of zie ladies' conversation."

The "whole party" followed the bright little docteur, who preceded them, throwing open the library door, then stepping briskly back with a profound bow to the ladies as they entered the more sociable apartment. There was quite a little bustle as everybody shook hands with Mark, who received the greetings with a cordial smile. Victor came gracefully forward, and by the time Lizbette's tray arrived the social ice was fairly broken. The stiff people lost some of their starch. Fat Mrs. Smith was laughing jollily, and Mr. Clark was talking so fast about botany, of which he knew nothing, and of Römer, of whom he actually had heard something, that Docteur Canonge could not keep pace with him comprehendingly, but he was making the most amiable though rather impotent attempts to reply with understanding and propriety. In one of his entangled sentences he broke down so plainly and so preposterously that even Natika's elegance and decorum gave way, and she burst out into an irrepressible, merry laugh over her grandfather's palpable mistakes, that was contagious. Docteur Canonge also laughed, and so did stiff Mr. Clark, while fat Mrs. Smith shook her fat sides like "a bowlful of jelly."

After a rather prolonged visit, the whole party took leave en masse as they had come, evidently pleased with the visit.

"Thank heaven, that's over!" said Natika, throwing herself exhausted into an easy-chair.

"I sink," said her grandfather, "zat children should be educated wiz knowledge of *conversation* as a social duty. It would ver' much lighten zie burden of life, if every soul met his fellow wiz frankness and amiable desire to please; and zis is matter of cultivation which Americans do much neglect."

"There seems to be a fierté in the English and American peoples," said Natika.

"A remnant of ancient savagery and isolation that has not been yet evolved out of them," put in Victor.

"Zey was a strong and fierce race, zose nordern peoples," said Docteur Canonge. "Zey were like zie carnivorous animals who seize zeir prey each for himself, and go off to zeir dens to devour it in silent peace. Zere still remains great inclination to division and individuation among zem which is not human, and truly not Christian."

"But, grandpapa, you know you are almost socialistic in *your* theories," said Victor.

"Perhaps! zere is someting of de Frenchman in me. Zie first impulse of zie Frenchman, when any proposition is made to him, is to say, 'I doubt.' Zey are a nation of doubters, true disciples of Descartes! Dey can nevare be very dogmatique because zey do nevare ver' strongly believe much. Zey can nevare see whole trutts anywhere; it is all half-trutts, and sometimes zey don't see noting true at all."

"They understand co-operation, though, and are ready to work and associate with others. So they have done much for science," said Mark.

"Yes, and all de great socialist theories have generally sprung out of French brains," replied the docteur. "I sink zey are probablement developed out of zose leetle tent-caterpillars who make a nation of zemselves, who form one huge tent on a single tree, who eat and sleep and make zeir diurnal promenades togedder every day."

"Grandpapa, Swedenborg says that the ordinary duties of society are to give 'breakfasts and dinners and suppers.' He has a long chapter about it," said Mark.

"Well, Swedenborg is right zere. It is always been considered a mark of amity to eat togedder among all nations in all periods of time. From zie earliest period among zie Hindoos, who are strict people of caste, zere has been zie highest honor awarded to Jagernath, whose festival drew zie largest crowd of pilgrims in zat ole world, by reason of de fact zat zere all zie people were equal, and zey all did eat togedder, zereby showing zie wide brotherhood of man. Jagernath have been ver' much calumniated idol. His car did nevare run over nobody, but have ever been zie symbol of love and fraternity among zie Hindoos. Zere is also zie traditional feasts of zie Scandinavians. Zey did eat togedder at Yule-tide and on oder times wen zie chiefs did assemble for council. And zere is zie old symbol of zie order of Freemasons—zie ver' name came from 'mas,' zie Gothic for 'a table.' Zey were band of brodders who do eat together all over zie world. And zere is zie higher mystery of zie mass, or zie Eucharist, among zie Christians. It is a remarkable fac' zat zie Divine Founder of our religion nevare invent nozing new by way of symbols. He take old sings and gave zem new and infinite meanings. He take zie washing of zie Hindoos and he turn it into baptism. He take zie fraternal feasts and he make it zie bond of union among all Christians, a sign of amity, equality, fraternity and true liberty."

"Oh, grandpapa! what would the priests say to hear you talk?" said Natika.

"Zey might say what zey like. I must trutt speak. I am Catolique out of respect to my ancestors and to my famille. But I make my own explanation of all zese matters to myself. I am a Christian, but I go much round a large circle of metaphysics before I get back to zie elementary mysteries, but I do get zere after while, and it contents me. I believe zie best I know, and zie most I can. But I see zere appears Mr. Antony Coolidge. He do come to see you, Natika, an' you can ver' well entertain one poor young man, wizout assistance from me or anybody," said Docteur Canonge, his eyes twinkling merrily. "So I will go again back to zie blouse and zie book-binding. I fear much my paste is all hard by zis time."

CHAPTER IX.

MONSIEUR LE DOCTEUR.

DOCTEUR CANONGE was extremely beloved in his neighborhood. He had a passion for his profession of medicine, and his tenderness and sympathy for his "poor patients" were ever ready and unfailing in all demands upon him.

Half the time he forgot to put down his medical calls in his books, and if a neighbor was cramped in his circumstances, the docteur's bill was never presented at all. When he received money, which he often did, he would thrust the bank notes into his pocket, where Lizbette would discover them woefully damaged by passing through the hands of the washerwoman who had charge of his usual costumes of linen or Attakapas cotonnade. It was only on grand occasions that the docteur appeared in the glory of black broadcloth, with all his ribands in his buttonholes. He had a pardonable small vanity in his ribands. They had been sent him by different scientific societies; and so "farouche" Republican as he was in principle, he valued the rewards of science above all things. When his brother Jacob, who had been so successful in accumulating money, reproached the docteur for his carelessness of what Jacob regarded as the chief end of life—"the making of money"—the docteur would shrug his shoulders up to his ears, and reply:

"What would you have, Jacob? I haf not zie talent to make much money; and zen I haf nevare had zie time cider; I haf been so busy in my life wiz oder sings, zat I had not any time at all! *You see I haf no time!*"

Jacob's "umph," sneering and contemptuous as it was, never affected the docteur's equanimity. He always persisted that he would have made a very great deal of money if he had had time to spare!

Docteur Canonge was the most tolerant of men, very patient of all men's idiosyncracies, which were a never ceasing study of deepest interest to him. Physically active, and so quick and restless as to be almost impatient, he was yet the very gentlest of human beings.

He was loyal, true, and deeply grateful in character. He had a very quick wit, that seemed sometimes to have a sting in its vivacity; but there was no root of bitterness in the man. The only thing he was not tolerant of was *intolerance*.

His religion was profound, but rather pantheistical. He read everything, from the Bhagavat Gita down to Comte and Herbert Spencer.

"Every man," he used to say, "makes for himself, according to the receptive power of his mind and senses, an image of zie universe, which, of course, decides his life here. We can see only so much as our eyes will perceive of anyzing. My idea of deity and zie universe must be an image, projected out of my own mind, not out of anozer mind. We can only make a guess at zie sum of probabilities. It is ver' foolish to dogmatize about anyzing. Trutt is like zie beautiful emerald bird in zie fairy tale, zat flies ever before us, enticing us to follow it to the more beautiful and better life. We can nevare seize it, but it is of great advantage zat we are led on. We learn; our souls expand. We enjoy larger life, fuller growth. We become grander beings; and all zie happiness we are capable of, we can find in zie *pursuit* of trutt; zie possession we can nevare have! Zie home of trutt is in zie bosom of deity! *Aspiration* and *power* of *growth*—zose are zie real joys of life; and it is mercifully provided zat we can nevare attain to positive trutt about nozing. As we grow, our planes of thought do widen, and we see zie light of knowledge streamen in on us from *all* sides, not *one* sides! I sink sometimes zat my mind's eye haf acquired as many facets as zat of a fly's eye. I see so many sides of trutt. I can only approach to trutt! I nevare can catch zat fairy bird."

Yet, with all his gentleness, Docteur Canonge was known to be a man of imperturbable coolness and of unfailing courage, both moral and physical. He had no sense of fear; but he ranked courage and integrity as simple elemental principles " of a gentleman." He considered it as a matter of course for *gentlemen* to be brave. Where he found the quality lacking, he treated it as an organic disease, or weakness of nerves, to be regarded as a serious malady.

He never had been known to quarrel with any one. But on one occasion, the son of a friend of his, visiting him, was very grossly insulted by a well-known Creole bully. The young man was what the old docteur called " a singularly *nervous* person." Other

people said he was a coward. At any rate the next
day, while the notorious bully was swaggering along
the public street, in the most frequented part of it,
he was met face to face by Docteur Canonge, who
stepped briskly along, carrying a small cowhide in
his hand. The docteur was bright, gay, smiling, as
he saluted the many friends who thronged the pave.
When he reached the bully, he stopped short and,
lifting his hat very courteously, he told him he
"had come to request an apology for his probably
unintentional affront to his (Docteur Canonge's)
guest." The bully glared at him with ineffable
contempt, and with a savage oath refused to make
"any apology." "I regret, then," said the little
docteur, "that I shall have to apply this!" Lifting
his hand quickly, he smote the infuriated duellist on
the face with his little riding-whip. With an ejacu-
lation the man sprang upon him; but the docteur
slipped nimbly aside, and brought down the whip
once more keenly upon the man's shoulders. A
crowd rushed in and separated the combatants.

The next day Docteur Canonge fought the bully
with small-swords and wounded him in the arm.
So soon as he had disabled him, Docteur Canonge
proffered his assistance to aid the surgeon in dress-
ing the wound. His adversary apologized to the
guest. Docteur Canonge spoke only once of the
affair. He said to an intimate friend, "Poor B——,
he is unfortunately of a very nervous temperament!

Of course, I had to fight for him! It was a necessity of honor. It is all matter of temperament! It is inconvenient to be nervous, as we have to live under zie code of honor here."

CHAPTER X.

A VERY WOMAN.

"NATIKA, what are you going to do with Antony?" asked Mark, looking quietly at Natika as she leaned forward, resting her head on her hand, waiting for the door bell to sound, as Antony neared the house after having fastened his horse to the rack at the side of the drive.

"*Do* with Antony Coolidge!" repeated Natika, indifferently. "Nothing, that I know. What is to be done with him, Mark? What possibilities lie infolded in that half-developed creature? that hybrid between races?"

"Oh, Natika," cried Mark, shocked at her levity, "what a shame to speak so lightly of a human soul which is lavishing its all of life and love at your feet! If a woman cannot respond, she should at least be grateful, and respect such love as that."

"Should she?" said Natika, carelessly. "Have you to learn, my cousin Mark, that 'should' and 'ought' are verbs that are not included in my vocabulary? I do not acknowledge any duties in life to anybody. I do exactly what I choose and what is according to my own will and pleasure. Do you remember Madame de Staël's excuse for herself? 'C'est ma nature ainsi.' Well, that's my creed. What I am, I am by birth, proclivities, accidents of life; and though I am deprived, from hatred of cant and hypocrisy, of many popular virtues, I retain one, of absolute truth to myself and also to those who are associated with me. What I am, I am; and I don't choose to be anything else. There's Mr. Coolidge's ring at the door. Now comes the announcement to me. Au revoir, messieurs! You are both rather wearisome with your sermonizing."

Natika kissed her hands most gracefully to her cousins; gathering all her little finger-tips to her rosy lips, then throwing out her hands towards them, scattering kisses as she ran gayly out of the room, the high heels of her satin slippers clattering lightly as she went.

"Take the heels off your slippers, Natika," called out Victor, "and walk noiselessly, like a lady."

"Like Panola, par exemple!" retorted Natika. "*My* ancestors did not steal upon their prey like wild beasts!"

Victor looked after her with a bitter smile upon his handsome lips. Mark looked after her with deep solicitude.

"No use, Mark!" exclaimed Victor. "It is the Venus Anadyomene! the creature made of foam of the sea! Capricious and merciless, like the treacherous wave, and—God help me!—maddening and fearful in her cruel beauty."

"It would be impossible to warn Antony," observed Mark, thoughtfully.

"*Impossible!* He would not believe you! God! *I know!*—and yet!"—Victor sprang up from his chair and paced up and down the room like a caged leopard. Mark looked at him pityingly.

"I can't understand it, Victor!" he said. "*I* love Natika truly! but *how* can you love her as you do, knowing her as you do?"

"Ask the moth why it flies to the candle, or the needle why it rushes to the loadstone," replied Victor, stopping before a window looking out on the garden, and then drumming upon the panes with his fingers. "It is all magnetism, I suppose, or something that science will explain some day or other, but not in time for me, or for Antony Coolidge, or a score of other fools like us. Mark, do you think one can overcome one love by cultivating another? Philosophers say vacuums are impossibilities. The only way to drive one love out of one's heart would be to crowd it out by another, I think."

"I don't know, but I think it might be wise to try," replied Mark, lightly.

"I have a half mind to try," said Victor; "I wish Chicora was younger and well, perhaps it would not be so difficult. There go Natika and Antony! Spoony fellow! What a dance she is leading him! They are gathering roses in the garden—thorns! Antony, take care of your poor, miserable fingers!—thorns to those flowers! Goodbye, Mark; I am going out for a gallop. I should like to gallop to the d——l, if I could."

Victor dashed out of the library, and Mark soon listened to his horse's clattering hoofs as he rushed past the library window, not halting even when he courteously lifted his hat, as he almost ran his horse past the parterre, where Natika was gathering flowers with Antony Coolidge, looking up into her eyes and hanging with passionate admiration upon her sweet, coquettish talk.

CHAPTER XI.

COUSINS' GOSSIP.

THE next day Mark heard Victor singing as he approached the study door in his quick, impulsive way. He sang an old romance of Rousseau's.

Victor's voice was delicious in its impassioned

9

depths. Mark heard it tremble, and he heard Natika laugh.

Natika and Victor came in together to Mark in the library. It was the custom of the house to go to Mark whenever any of the inmates went out and returned laden with fresh gossip, or any more substantial gifts for Mark, who had grown to be the fixed centre of all the family-life and interests. Indeed, Mark Bolling was most tenderly regarded by the whole community of his grandfather's friends, so that he used to say, laughingly, "that life had always its compensations." He had a grateful, sensitive nature, and was responsive to, and appreciative of, every little grain of kindness or happiness that was brought to him.

Natika brought him now a magnificent Japanese lily, which she held up under his nose.

"There! ain't that a beauty! I got it from Madame Bolling's garden, and brought it carefully home for you."

"It is splendid!" said Mark, taking the superb flower from her hand. "So you and Victor have been to call at my stepmother's."

"Yes, and who do you think we found domesticated there? Who but Miss Clark! the shy, the awkward, the huge—"

"And the pretty!" put in Victor.

"Yes, she *is* pretty," replied Natika, carelessly. "She has really a beautiful face, but it is of no use to her; it is a great *waste*, beauty on such a woman as that."

"She is rather 'vast' in her proportions," said Victor. "She would have filled the Scandinavian idea of a wife for Thor or Odin!—she is so big altogether."

"Not quite six feet," continued Natika; "well made, too, if she knew how to manage herself; very pretty hair, that she does not keep tidy; very pretty hands, that are not immaculately clean; quite a sweet voice, which she strains horribly, and fine clothes that fit her not at all; she wears her clothes as if they were hung upon a clothes-horse; she does not drape herself at all. I really feel sorry for Nature when I find her excellent gifts so squandered."

"You are severe," said Mark; "what has poor Miss Clark done to you?"

"Made love to Antony Coolidge," said Victor, quietly. "It is funny to see how she makes eyes at Antony. Natika considers that as an interference with her prerogative. She never allows any other woman to interfere with her slaves, or to have or to keep a lover in her presence."

Natika laughed, and flashed a bright, bewildering glance upon Victor.

"It is delightful to have such a well-trained and intelligent cousin as Victor. He is *so* intelligent and helpful. It is very comfortable for me."

Victor bit his lip. He always came out worsted from an encounter with Natika.

"The truth is, Mark, la grande et belle Miss Clark *is* in love with Antony. Isn't it curious? Such creatures as women do fancy! I don't believe Shakespeare exaggerated one particle when he made Titania in love with Bottom. Antony Coolidge is a psychological study to me; that's the reason *I* suffer him. Hasn't he queer eyes? they are just like those of a cuttle-fish! they protrude so much, and are so watery and pale-colored."

"A cuttle-fish is very sensitive," said Mark; "it blushes all over when irritated, and suffers. It even covers itself with erected papillæ. I have pity for cuttle-fish; they seem to have more sentient and conscious life than other fishes."

"Perhaps they have," replied Natika, with non-chalance. "I suppose they also have a keener sense of enjoyment than calmer fishes, so it is all balanced. I declare, Madame Bolling is very charming; she is a good study of fine color."

"What a true Greek you are, Natika!" said Mark, smiling; "a real sensuous Greek."

"I like a perfect mind in a perfect body," said Natika, gravely, leaning her elbows on the table and her chin upon her elegantly-gloved hands, and looking steadily at Mark; "I don't often find it."

"No one, and nothing will ever satisfy you," exclaimed Victor.

"Perhaps not. I think I might have loved Alcibiades—perhaps Pericles, or Columbus," said she, laughing. "There's not a man among the Romans who would have attracted me. They are too one-sided, and too stern."

"Wouldn't you have liked Antony? I mean Mark Antony, not Antony Coolidge."

"No. Antony drank too much, and was not intellectual enough for me. I think if Socrates had been handsomer I might have fancied *him*. However, Mark, you should have witnessed how Miss Clark was bourgeoning and blossoming under the melting influence of Antony's charms. She *talked*, absolutely *talked*, in a ceaseless, perpetual flow of exceedingly uninteresting platitudes; an inexhaustible dribble that was nearly prostrating to ordinary human intelligences. I did wish myself transformed into a rock, or a deaf mute, or anything to escape from it; once the floodgate lifted off her silence, the infinitely small source appears to be exhaustless. But Victor amiably sacrificed himself, and Antony was flattered, as men always are."

Victor laughed.

"Merci for my sex," said Mark, smiling.

"I always except *you*, Mark," said Natika, gathering up her drapery. "I must go take off my hat."

CHAPTER XII.

CHICORA'S FAWN.

MARK had a fine talent for drawing and a good eye for color, a gift of nature in which he found great delight, and which he had cultivated carefully both at home and in Europe. He often spent whole days absorbed before his easel, which had been carefully contrived so as to move readily by mechanism, that he might reverse the usual order of a painter's motions, for instead of rising and walking back from his easel in order to judge of an effect, poor Mark would shove the whole apparatus off from him, controlling its movements by cords and pulleys until he got the desired focus for his eyes It was rather cumbrous, but he had learned immense patience, and was very grateful for any means by which the monotony and helplessness of his life could be relieved. All of his small circle took the deepest interest in everything that interested him, so that his paintings were subjects of comment and affectionate observation from their inception to their finishing. Panola especially used to be never weary of sitting by his side to watch his skilful touches, and used to make superwomanly efforts to provide him with graceful subjects for his pencil. She would bring him flowers, leaves, weeds, etc., for his foregrounds; would sit immovably hour after hour for the innumerable sketches Mark would make of herself in every conceivable poetic or allegorical pose. Mark painted all of his friends— Natika, Victor, his grandfather, Lizbette, Cherokee Joe, his stepmother, every body that would sit to him, and no one ever refused to do anything that could give Mark pleasure. So he had all of them.

Victor was rummaging one day in Mark's studio, when he came across a half-finished picture which struck his fancy, and he asked Mark to explain the design. He recognized the likenesses.

It was a fine portrait of Chicora. She was represented as sitting in a grove of noble trees, upon a low bank covered with grass; leaning against her shoulder, with one arm encircling her mother's graceful neck, was the little two-year-old Panola, white as a snowflake; just the pale little child Victor remembered, looking whiter in contrast with the rich roseate tintings of her mother's flesh. Chicora was beautiful, with a warmth of color that Titian would have rejoiced over; she was represented in her early youth, in the fullest splendor of her life-loveliness. Victor felt a rush of admiration that amounted to a pang of pain as he looked upon the quiet picture and recalled the present condition of this transcendently lovely woman. The eyes of the picture, though large and lustrous in their midnight blackness, had not the expression of defiance and concentrated vitality that they now wore perpetually. In the picture they were soft and tender as a Madonna's. The infant Panola stood upon one side of her mother, and upon the other, with one foot laid upon Chicora's lap and the other lifted playfully pawing in the air as if to attract her attention, was a noble red deer, his antlers showing that he was only about two years old. The deer was licking Chicora's hand, as she encircled Panola's waist and pressed the child closer to her maternal breast.

"What a beautiful picture!" exclaimed Victor. "What does it mean?"

"Oh, that!" replied Mark, pausing from his work to glance up; "that is Chicora and her children. Did you never hear of Panola's foster-brother, the wild deer?"

"No," said Victor; "what about it?"

"When Panola was two or three months old Chicora was nourishing her from her own breast, and was in danger of suffering from the too abundant secretion of milk. Grandpapa proposed she should adopt another infant for a while, but there were only little negro children to be found, and Chicora could not subdue her repugnance to the race, so grandpapa was much troubled, when one day Cherokee Joe brought into Chicora's chamber a young fawn of two days age, whose dam he had shot. Chicora took the poor little beast, and it fed from her bosom until it got old enough to feed itself, dividing her cares with Panola. It was really touching to see the creature's love for Panola and Chicora; it would crawl upon the couch by the child and lie down by her when she was sleeping, and lick her hands and feet; when it grew older it would never suffer a stranger to approach Panola: it would spring into an attitude of defiance, and stamp its hoofs and shake its head, already adorned with soft antlers. It followed Chicora everywhere; would lie down at her feet, and showed a wondrous docility and intelligence; somehow it seemed to have imbibed a sort of human instinct from Chicora's milk. It lived for several years, and when it died Major Flanoy had it buried. I began to paint that picture for him, but he died suddenly, and I never completed it."

"I wish you would finish it for me," exclaimed Victor. "It is so pretty and so queer! I don't wonder Panola has so much of the wild fawn about her, since she had such a companion in her infancy. Somehow it does not seem incongruous in Chicora, her preferring the deer of the wild woods to an African baby."

"No," replied Mark; "there remains under all the cultivation of Chicora and Panola a strain of wildness and primeval shyness and reticence."

"Do you know, I find that immensely attractive," said Victor.

"It is because you are a true creature of the salon

you appreciate a touch of true, wild nature," said Mark, smiling.

"Will you complete the picture for me?" asked Victor, not replying to Mark's words, but gazing on the picture intensely. It fascinated him.

"Yes, with pleasure."

"Thanks. I shall value it. It is the reverse of the story of Genevieve of Brabant, is it not?"

"Yes, the dove fed Genevieve, but Chicora fed the deer," said Mark.

"She is close kin to primeval nature anyhow," said Victor, "and she—is very beautiful."

NOTE BY AUTHOR.—This incident of suckling a fawn by a Southern lady is taken from real life.

CHAPTER XIII.

A SAGE'S PHILOSOPHY.

"GRANDPAPA," exclaimed Natika, one day when they were all gathered, as usual, about Mark in the study; "grandpapa, do you call yourself a Comtist?" she glanced at the book which her grandfather was reading—it was "Comte's Philosophy."

"No," replied the docteur, looking up from his page, meditatively. "I do not call myself anyzing as yet, Natika. I zink I should razer be classed in a ver' general and wide classification among zie order of zie Christians; of course, perhaps of a peculiar species."

Victor laughed aloud. "A *very* peculiar species, I think, grandpapa," he said.

The old man looked at him gravely, then after a moment's silence he said:

"My chief object in life is to search after the truth, wherever it may be found. I cannot zay I haf found more zan I really haf done. My powers and senses are very limited. I have studied not wiz pride, neider arrogance, but wiz deep humilitee, and great willingness to learn, in any way, some little truth from anybody at all. I have immense sympathie wiz aspiration after perfection, anywhere and anyhow. Wherever life is, I find zat life wonderful, miraculous, mysterious—an atom in zie Divine, a part in zie Infinite! I have *immense* respeck for all life, for zie ordered Kosmos, for zie creative power; zat I admire, I reverence, I adore, I love!"

The old man put his hands gently together, as if in prayer, as he spoke, and his eyes glowed, his thin face became radiant, and a slight flush crept over his sallow cheeks. He bowed his head reverently as he uttered the last words. His grandchildren looked at him with tender, respectful eyes. The intense earnestness with which he spoke was most impressive. The old man paused and then continued:

"I know not much. I have been able to formulate but little of a system of religion for myself. I find zie essential truths whose highest utterance has come from zie lips of Jesus Christ. I find someting of zose truths in all periods, and in all zie high teachings of zie world from pre-historic times. I like not names; I like not partisanship; I like not zie narrow teachings of theology anywhere; I like not too much definition. I love zie good everywhere; I love zie truth everywhere; I love what you call God, zie all Fader; I love man. I reverence life and organization, mental, physical and moral. I zink zere has not been any teacher like Jesus; I zink he had more of zie divine life in his manhood dan any ozer. So far, he has taught zie best I know. I like zie Christ spirit; it is zie right spirit, zie divine spirit. I zink I am pretty much of a Christian, Natika."

"Grandpapa, are you a Pantheist, then?" asked Victor.

"No," said Mark, "he is rather what Krause calls a '*pan-en-theist*'—not 'en-kai-pan,' but 'pan-en-theo.'"

"Your distinctions are too subtle for me," said Victor, yawning.

Natika looked at Victor half contemptuously, and pityingly.

"Your brain is too light for metaphysics," she said.

"Natika has the brain of the Greek; it is subtle and mobile," said Docteur Canonge, smilingly.

CHAPTER XIV.

THE ASTRONOMICAL CALCULATION.

"MARK, I wish I was as calm and equable as you are," exclaimed Victor, after he had been spending an hour in trying to read a French novel, in restlessly marching up and down the room, in snapping his fingers by pulling the knuckle-bones out suddenly, and then allowing them to relapse into their joints, in whistling and humming snatches of favorite arias, and in watching Natika's white hands as they moved lightly and gracefully over her embroidery frame, for this morning Natika had been seized with a fit of industry and domesticity.

"I really *should* like you to be a little less restless, Victor," replied Mark, with a good-humored smile; "at least until I complete this calculation for grandpapa—an astronomical one that goes into differential calculus, and is not so very easy for me to make."

"Easy enough for grandpapa," said Natika. "Why don't he make it himself?"

"He has not time to-day," said Mark, quietly. "I like to aid him, and it is very good in him to accept of my poor help sometimes."

Natika glanced at her cousin with a flash in her eye, then smiled as she said merrily:

"'Get thee behind me, Satan!' I wish you would not *always* be so irreproachable, Mark. It is really fatiguing to have to keep up with so much virtue and goodness."

"'And the Athenians grew weary of hearing Aristides called the Just,'" sententiously quoted Victor from Grecian history.

"Behold Saul among the Prophets!" retorted Natika.

"Natika," said Victor, gravely, "you are a very exhausting person. You are worse than quicksilver. You are never at rest. You are an incarnated kaleidoscope; you can converse on any subject with an awful Greek loquacity. You inherit all this from your ancestors. Why don't you imbibe tranquillity from Mark or—Panola?"

"Panola!" exclaimed Natika, scornfully; "Panola! am I to take lessons in deportment from a—" Natika hesitated; she caught Mark's eye fixed gravely upon her. "Well; *you* are part Indian yourself, Mark," she concluded, half apologetically.

"Yes," said Mark, "I have no doubt Panola and I both owe much of our power of self-control to our aboriginal forefathers. I, for one, am very thankful to them for the quality—even if I appear somewhat stolid and impassive."

"It is a good coating of armor against the 'stings and arrows of outrageous fortune,'" said Victor; "or even against Natika's shafts of Attic wit and sarcasm."

"Don't be silly," said Natika; "it bores me!"

"Why do you 'bore' Natika?" exclaimed Docteur Canonge, emerging from his laboratory with an open book in his outstretched hand. "Good-morning, my dearest children. You are well and happy to-day, I trust?" The old man embraced his granddaughter and kissed her; then in his affectionate French way he kissed his grandsons each upon the forehead, as was his morning custom in greeting them. "I am rather late this morning," he continued, "but I was up nearly all night watching the transit of a star, and I overslept myself; but I have gained someting! I have discovered a mistake of five seconds in Moedler's calculations. I shall proceed immediately to acquaint him with it. You have finish the calculation, Mark? I did wish to verify mine with yours."

Mark handed the paper he had been calculating to his grandfather. The old man cast his eye rapidly over the columns of figures: his face glowed.

"It is correc'; I have right; it is full five seconds zat Moedler was wrong! I zank you ver' much, Mark!"

"Pshaw! grandpapa!" said Natika, biting off the end of her floss to thread her needle. "What great difference would five seconds make anyhow?"

"Five seconds of time iu a transit!" exclaimed Docteur Canonge. "Five seconds—zat is a great deal! It make difference of many zousand miles in de distance of a star!"

Natika put up her red lips and smiled. "If it pleases you, grandpapa," she said, softly, in flute-like tones, "it is well!"

"You do not care so much for science, Natika," said Docteur Canonge.

"I care for you, dear grandpapa," replied the siren in her gentlest dove-notes—there were exquisite cadences in Natika's voice when she chose to use them.

"What book have you got there in your hand?" she continued, wishing to please her grandfather.

"Zis is de 'Bhagrat Gita,' the great hymn of god of ze Hindoos—zat is de meaning of Bhagrat: Bhaga, god—gita, poem or song. It is de Bible of ze Hindoo. An' ver' good Bible, I zink."

"Grandpapa!" exclaimed Natika, holding up her hands, "grandpapa, what will the curé say to that?"

Docteur Canonge shrugged his shoulders. "I

care not for what he will say ; I zink what I zink! In zis book I find ze germs of most modern theology. It is not less ze truth because it was also known to zose Hindoos before ze day of Moise. I have *great* respek for Moise, but I zink he learn much from ze Egyptians, who did also learn all zey did know from zose Hindoos."

Natika laughed and clapped her hands. "Grandpapa, you would have been excommunicated and burnt up by the good Catholics of the middle ages!"

"Probablement ; but I zink I keep ze true essence of ze Christian faith ; so I care not for ze mint and ze cumin of small dogmas. I shall tell you a story, Natika."

"Why don't you say 'narrative,' grandpapa?" said Victor, gayly laughing. "You never heard that story, Natika. Grandpapa had a French friend here who wished to learn English, and grandpapa undertook to teach him. Grandpapa explained to him that a story, a tale, and a narrative meant all the same thing. So the pupil undertook one day to tell an anecdote of a long-tailed monkey; and he called it a 'very much narratived monkey,' so we got the joke on grandpapa!"

Docteur Canonge laughed merrily. "It is all true, Natika. Zis shall be, however, not 'a very *much* narrative,' but a short tale of my monkey."

10

CHAPTER XV.

THE STORY OF ODIN.

"THERE lived in the rich garden land of the world, which lies at the foot of the Himalayas, a great king, the first of all mankind, the wisest and the noblest. This great king was named Arya, and he had many sons and daughters, until the land of Paradise became too short and too narrow for them all to dwell in. So he called them one by one to his presence, and he gave them gifts and he sent them away to seek other lands and new Paradises; and they went forth weeping, bearing costly gifts of gold and pearl and silken garments fine as the woven wind; and they found new homes, some near by, some farther off from their father's house; and at last all were sent away but the youngest and the eldest born, who was to be king after his father. And finally, the youngest was to go, and his father gave him snow-white horses, and a golden circlet for his head, and bands of gold upon his arms, and he also gave to him, besides the garments of silk, other wrappings of wool and fur; for Odin, that was his name, had to go far, far away beyond the homes of his elder brothers, who had built up royal cities in all the lands they had taken possession of. That was all King Arya had to give to Odin, his youngest son, besides the strong bow and arrow, and the battle-axe of stone, which Arya had used to slay tigers and elephants with. Years and years now passed away. Arya was gathered to his fathers, and his eldest son reigned in his stead. Ages fled. The family of the great king still lived in the garden land of the Himalayas. They lived as they had ever lived, keeping up all the old traditions of the father land, and the Paradise grew poor and barren from the over-populousness, and the growth of rusty superstitions which overspread the minds of its inhabitants. Occasionally they would hear of, or hold intercourse with, their relatives who had settled in the gardens of Persia and Assyria and Egypt, and even still further in Greece and Rome. They never forgot their kinship. Indeed, it told itself in the likeness of the peoples, in their habits, language, religions. There were wonderful dramas enacted in this great family of the descendants of King Arya. But they never heard of the fate of the youngest born, the beloved Odin. He was supposed to be lost and entombed among the polar snows and ice. Ages passed, and still the family of the elder brother Hindus lived, half-sleeping, in their hot old ancestral home, when suddenly there came a lightning flash which circled round the earth."

"Telegraph," whispered Victor to Natika. Docteur Canouge smiled and nodded his head.

"A lightning flash which startled them from their slumber. It brought greetings from the sons of Odin to their brethren. They had wrestled with nature in their cold northern home until they had won priceless gifts and secrets from her, and they came now, bearing all these precious gifts of science and art, of wisdom and skill, back to clasp the hands of their brothers, and thus to close the great golden circle of humanity, the glorious bond of family life amongst the children of the great King Arya. And they also brought back fully developed and much changed the traditions of their early faith. They gave into the hands of their brethren, instead of this book—"

Docteur Canonge took up his book and smoothed it gently with one hand while he spoke: "They gave to *them—descendants* of this book—they gave them the Zenda Vista, and the Koran, and the Hebrew Scriptures, and the Greek and Syriac Testament, and all the civilizations and all the knowledge that had grown out of all these, and instead of the circlet of gold the children of Odin wore—"

"Silk and beaver hats!" said Victor.

"Bonnets and plumes!" said Natika.

"Casques of mail and war feathers!" said Mark.

"No," said Docteur Canonge. "Ye Indians of America were not Aryans—not 'war feathers,' but 'casques of mail.' Yes, perhaps!

"And they walked on the sea with white-winged

ships, and carried thunder and lightning in their pockets (pistols, you know), and ran express trains with smoking, chained, and fettered dragons," said Victor, laughing.

"Grandpapa, that is a lovely narrative," exclaimed Natika, throwing her arms about the old man's neck and kissing him. "And I shall always ever hereafter respect the old family Bible, the Bhagavat Gita."

Docteur Canonge pressed Natika to his bosom, and went off with his book held aloft in triumph above his bald head. Mark called after him timidly. Mark disliked so much to shake his grandfather's confidence in himself. But he summoned up courage to say now what he had been thinking. 'Grandpapa, did you make allowance for 'personal equation' in seeing that transit?"

Docteur Canonge stopped short, put down his book, smiled in a curious, puzzled, half-ashamed way. Then he pulled out his snuff-box, took a pinch out of it, and said slowly and half-reluctantly:

"No, I don't—believe I did!"

Mark looked down at his own figures on the paper,—"Would not it be *better* to—"

"Yes," interrupted the docteur, "of course it will be better; perhaps Moedler is not so far wrong as five seconds after all."

CHAPTER XVI.

LOVE WILL RULE.

DOCTEUR CANONGE was greatly troubled in mind about Mark. He thought that Mark had been so cruelly treated by his brother's will that it seemed as if the kind old man sought in every possible way to give expression to his own tenderness for his afflicted grandson. Mark felt this, and exerted himself as much as possible to be cheerful and even gay, for fear of his grandfather's suspecting him of brooding over what was indeed a disappointment, for Mark felt most bitterly his helpless dependence upon the active but feeble old man, who lived up to his small income, and whose only regret was that he had no more to give; and as yet there did not appear any possibility of relief from this heavy dependence for poor Mark. Mark would have gladly changed places with the healthy Irish ditcher, whom he saw digging away at the earth, and wheeling his scrapers full of dirt in building up the great levees.

One morning Docteur Canonge proposed at the breakfast table that Mark should make one more trial for the recovery of the use of his limbs by going again to the Arkansas hot springs for a few weeks. When he was there before he got so much better that he could stand upon his feet, though still unable to walk; but the hot vapor baths, while they seemed to benefit him in one respect, had weakened him so much in others, that the resident physician had advised his leaving the place and abandoning the use of the waters.

Natika listened, while her grandfather passed his eulogium on the wonderful effects of the hot and mud baths, and then said she believed she would go too, as the vapor baths had great cosmetic power. Natika had spied a small pimple on her face, and she fancied that if there were any humors in the skin, she would get rid of them by these vapor baths. Mark was willing to please his grandfather, though he had little hope himself of any great benefit; the surgeons had told him so repeatedly that no *external* impulse or application would be of any avail to him, that the circulation of the interrupted nerve force must come from *internal* matter, that the impulse must proceed directly from his *own brain*.

"One powerful rush of life-force might do it," said they.

Victor was piqued at Natika's making her plans independently of him, so he played with his teaspoon on the edge of his cup, while the others were discussing their preliminary arrangements, and when his grandfather alluded to him as being of course included in the proposed party for the jaunt, he electrified the small company by declaring that he for one had no fancy for the trip, and preferred to remain where he was. "Lizbette would take care of him," he said, "and he should go shooting with Cherokee Joe, play billiards with young Smith, and go to see Miss Panola and her mother."

Natika's eyes flashed when she heard this defiant proclamation of his independence; but she knew him too well to press the matter, or to say anything to change his resolution. She knew Victor would weary sooner than she would of their separation. So she kept silence while Docteur Canonge and Mark expostulated with Victor and tried to persuade him to change his resolution, and to accompany the party. Like all weak natures with strong desires and of infirm impulses Victor was very jealous of the appearance of being influenced by others. He thought it showed a strong mind and was manly to stick to his own way, even when reason would show him that the way of others was probably better than his. He had no real principles, but he was very obstinate in opinions and in small matters. Natika understood him thoroughly. She often had some contempt for him mingled with her real affection for him, which latter was as much the growth of habit and gratification of the sense of power as a real preference for Victor. If she had real preference for any human being it was for Mark, not Victor. Victor remained inflexible in his determination: to the Arkansas springs he would *not go*.

Just as the party arose from the table and Mark was wheeled into his study, the door bell rang, and Antony Coolidge was announced. He had come by appointment to drive out with Natika. Victor looked gloomily after her as she drove past the window of Mark's room. Seeing him standing she kissed her hand gracefully to him in token of adieu. The loveliest smile shone upon her face. She was imperturbable in her good humor. Victor looked after the buggy as it vanished in the distance, and then, turning away from the window with a muttered curse, threw himself down in a chair near Mark, who was reading as usual. Mark looked up. Victor was sitting with his head buried in his hands.

"Victor," said Mark, laying down his book, "Victor, there are only us three cousins to care for each other in this world—that is, of our own family. I have the love of a brother for you and for Natika. May I use the freedom of a brother and speak out frankly to you?"

"Say any thing you please," said Victor, bitterly. "I don't promise that I shall take any advice you may please to proffer. I don't like advice, but I will listen to what you have to say, if that suits you."

"Well, what I have to say is this, dear Victor. You love Natika?"

"Yes," bitterly said Victor.

" Does she return your love?"

" No." This was scornfully said by Victor.

" Then why waste your whole life in this useless pursuit of a woman who does not love you?"

" Because I can't help it. Because Natika is my fate. Do you suppose I have not struggled? Do you suppose I like to be the slave of this woman's whims and caprices? Again and again I have said to myself all and more than you can possibly say to me on this subject. I have kept away; I have tried dissipations, other scenes, and have always gone back to her, and I know I always shall. Natika is the curse of my life and yet all the joy of it."

" Victor, what I am going to say to you is more important to you than even the moral objections you may have urged against love for Natika. You ought not to marry Natika, even if she were willing. My reasons are solely medical ones. I have watched you both carefully, and I tell you now that both Natika and yourself are inclined to be consumptive, and that if you marry, the lungs of the weaker one, whichever it may be, will certainly fail, and one will die. I have observed this fact so frequently. I have so often seen the weak lungs of the husband relieved by the wife taking his disease from him and perishing in consequence, and vice versa. Now I forewarn you, that will be your fate, for Natika is stronger than you are, and if you marry, *she* will be your death unconsciously."

"So be it," said Victor, sombrely. "I have been told this before. A gypsy said as much once when we had our fortunes told in England. She told me my love for Natika would cause my death. I expect it will some way or other, but I think I shall blow my brains out some day. I won't wait to die of consumption."

"Oh, Victor!" ejaculated Mark, truly shocked at the light manner of his cousin. "Oh, Victor! God forbid!"

"Needs must when the devil drives," replied Victor. "What a stupid fool Antony Coolidge is! Poor moth, to burn himself in that flame. I could find it in my heart to grieve for Antony. I know where he will end: in the bottom of the bayou, or in the mad house, or in the inebriate asylum, or on the end of a rope. Alas, for Antony! He is in the net of the Cleopatra who will only laugh and mock at him, and fling him off when she is wearied, as a child does a squeezed orange."

CHAPTER XVII.

HOT SPRINGS OF ARKANSAS.

"MY DEAR VICTOR:

It was quite a pleasure to hear from you again, and to learn that you were so happy in the society of Miss Flanoy and the other fair damsels of the campagne. I delivered your messages to grandpapa and to Mark. They were obliged for your remembrance of them. I don't think Mark is improving at all in health, though grandpapa is very reluctant to concede the fact; and Mark is so very patient and considerate that he is not willing to destroy suddenly the airy fabric built up by grandpapa's sanguine hopefulness. Mark is weaker than he was, and I think he will have soon to give up the use of these powerful baths. I have been taking them moderately. Undoubtedly they are great cosmetics, for I never had such roses and lilies in my face before. I am very glad I came, for it is a good preparation for my winter campaign in Paris.

"This is a rough but interesting place. The country must have been of volcanic origin. There are innumerable hot springs; I believe, more than eighty on this low mountain, sending up steam and vapor continually. The water is hot enough to boil an egg in, and there are places where beautiful crystals of rock quartz are found, and great quantities of magnetic loadstones; plenty of white limestones, with red veins through it, almost marble in hardness. I found a beautiful piece with an exquisite fossil leaf in it yesterday. There is also sandstone here, and jet. Onyx and large garnets are also found.

" There are many guests here, chiefly composed of invalids. It is rather a Bethesda, but one always finds somebody worth seeing and talking to. I have not been yet ennuiee. I have a good deal of amusement in watching Mark. All the women here are taken with him, and it is funny to see how they run after him. There are several here that I call ' his train,' who never let him have a moment's peace, they are so devoted. It is a study to me, who, you know, am rather accustomed to see things done differently, that is, to see men éperdus for women. It teases Mark a good deal. But he is gentle and polite. I tell him he is gently cruel to his adoratcuses. They seem to be on the watch for him; they time their meals to suit his; they bring him wild flowers (which are extremely beautiful here); they bring him offerings of crystals and jet, and all sorts of stones and weeds and leaves and fruits. They read the most tender poems to him. They write him feeble verses. They watch his face. They exist only in the sunshine of his smile. One of them, rather an old girl, who wears spectacles and does up the principal literary characters, is perversely jealous, even of *me!* I think, according to your transmigration theory, she was evolved through the frogs ; she has that sort of a face. Mark is getting tired of it. He does not like the painful rank of a beau in society. I think he will soon persuade grandpapa to go home.

"I have just had a letter from the Reads, in New York. They sail soon for Europe. I think I shall join them. There is a family going from this place to New York next week. So I shall probably not return to Louisiana with grandpapa and Mark. If you should be in Paris next winter, you will probably find me, as usual, at my cousin, Madame Ronher's. I expect I shall meet you some day unexpectedly on the drive of the Bois de Boulogne, jusqu'a cetteheure de ravissement. I am, dear Victor, your cousin and friend,   NATIKA.

"P. S.—Antony Coolidge has been here a week. He begins to be tiresome. Mark has just rolled himself out to my side on this verandah, where I am writing ; and here appear the train also. It is astonishing, the necessity of ordinary women for something to gush over upon. They must expend the overflow of sentiment in their tender bosoms, whether it be on parrots, or poodles, or men. For my part I prefer poodles, though you never had any patience with Faufan. She likes the warm baths here very much. I take her in every day. It is good for her health."

" I wonder why women like Natika are so satirical towards their own sex," thought Victor. " The two women I know best, she and Panola, are certainly not given ' to gush,' as she calls it. God knows she is as changeable as a chameleon and very difficult to keep pleased with anything ; that is just her charm. And Panola is cold as an iceberg. It would be interesting to thaw her snow. She is far the nobler woman. But then Natika is so cursedly fascinating. Other women are *so* commonplace beside her!"

CHAPTER XVIII.

IN THE DARK HOURS.

VICTOR managed to occupy his days in shooting, fishing, driving and riding. The evenings he generally spent at Mrs. Flanoy's. He asked permission of her to come there freely, appealing to her charity for relief from loneliness, or the society of old Lizbette. Mrs. Flanoy liked Victor. She was pleased to have him come to see her. She liked his singing and his graceful, pleasant ways. Panola liked him, too, and was grateful to him for his evident admiration of her mother, and for the care he took to please Mrs. Flanoy.

Music was a great bond between Panola and Victor; and then Victor was Mark's cousin, and he resembled Mark a good deal. It was pleasant to look at eyes so like to Mark's in color and shape, though they differed in expression. And it was something novel to the young Panola to receive from a young man all the graceful little courtesies which their constant intercourse enabled Victor to proffer to her when they were so much together, and very often alone together. It was impossible for a man of sentiment not to be sometimes rather more tender in voice and manner than occasion seemed to necessitate. It was natural impulse between the sexes.

Victor had no intention of making love to Panola, but he did it, and sometimes he cursed himself for doing it. For, however he might amuse himself with other women, he *knew* that his inner heart never failed in its deep habit of allegiance to Natika. With all her faults, she was the one and only woman he really desired on the earth. Her indifference and coquetry only rivetted his chains the closer, because it made any consummation of his hopes so very uncertain. He was angry with Natika. He said to himself a thousand times that he *would* not follow

her back to Paris. He repeated it the oftener that he
distrusted his own resolution. If Natika should
write him one single tender or flattering line, he
knew he should certainly be a passenger on the next
steamer for Havre. Yet he tried to make himself
in love with Panola. There were hours in which
he fancied he had partially succeeded.

The magnetic power of her mother over him he
fully recognized. If Chicora had been well and in
any condition to justify such a feeling, Victor suspected it just possible that *she* might inspire him
with a passion almost as powerful as that which he
felt for Natika. But Panola, in all the splendor of
her beauty, never would! Yet he had a sort of
jealous dislike at the thought of any other man's
ever possessing Panola. He did not want her himself, but he did not want anybody else to have her.
So his conduct became fitful and capricious towards
Panola. The young girl's manner never varied
much. She was always calm, cold, and loftily courteous to Victor. She liked him best when he was
simply a *bon camarade* in his manner towards herself. For, when he paid her lover-like attentions,
Panola felt as if a sort of ice-crust slowly formed
itself over her heart. The touch of his hand, if it
pressed hers, did not warm her, but produced a sensation of torpidity and an impulse of repulsion.

When Mark and his grandfather returned, they
found Victor still living at Docteur Canonge's; but

11

after they had been home a week, Victor suddenly departed for New Orleans, and they did not hear from him for several months.

About this time the Confederate war broke out, and when next they heard from Victor, he was enlisted in the southern army and had got a commission on a general's staff. In his letter he mentioned casually that he had a letter from Natika; that she was engaged to be married to an " Italian marchese." "But," wrote Victor, "Natika's being *engaged* is no positive certainty that she will ever marry this man! She has been engaged before this. Antony Coolidge is gone to the dogs. The foolish fellow followed Natika abroad, was scornfully dismissed by her, and he has just given himself up to the wildest sort of a life. He is as often in the gutters as anywhere else. He has no power of resistance or of recuperation in him. Once the rein given to the neck of his ungovernable appetites, which were the poor fellow's inheritance with his mixed blood, he is gone. He is *here*. I have tried to do what I could for him, but it has ended in nothing. The quicker the misery and the degradation is over for him, the better. The man was not devoid of good qualities if Natika had let him alone. He is good-natured and docile, and rather affectionate; but his passion for Natika has unloosed the hyena in his nature, and now his appetites for wickedness and debauchery and the lowest sensual indulgences are insatiable!

His mother had better come to look after him. She can stay him in his mad career of wicked folly. I have written frankly to her, for as much as I dislike her I suppose she has some maternal instincts left."

Victor's letter must have produced its effect, for Madame Bolling quitted the Pavilion and went off to her son. She did not return for several months. When she came back she was robed in mourning; her son had died by his own hand in a fit of mania potu. Madame seemed to be very much distressed. It was doubtless a grief to her. She had schemed and plotted, perhaps had committed crimes to advance the interests of her son, and he had despised her counsels and mocked at her wishes. He had forsaken Panola and gone madly after Natika, who laughed at him.

Madame was very pale when she returned to the Pavilion. It was well, perhaps, that the ocean rolled between Natika and this sorely-afflicted mother, for Madame Bolling was not a woman to sit down patiently or resignedly under a real or a fancied injury. She always had found some means of vengeance on her foes, but she knew the great virtue of patience. Madame used to say, "the one needful quality in this world was *patience to wait* for opportunity." "The world is round, and it turns, and people meet," she used to quote from the Italian. So she returned to cultivate her little gar-

den and to be sweetly amiable to her niece and to
her disagreeable sister-in-law, who never permitted
her to enter into her apartment. Mrs. Flanoy was
very positive in her prejudices, and her daughter
and servants had long before learned the inflexibility
of her will.

The war surged around the quiet neighborhood.
All the young men had gone into the army. Mark
chafed more and more against his helplessness.
Half the Cherokees, with Satana at their head, had
joined the Confederate army under General Albert
Pike, of Arkansas.

Year after year rolled on until the last eventful
one, when the contest was being ended so far as open
fighting went.

CHAPTER XIX.

MARRIED IN HASTE.

ACCIDENTAL circumstances brought Victor
once more near his grandfather, and it was
but natural that he should seek to see the old gentleman. Mark and the old docteur were delighted
to see him, one fine spring morning, enter the well-
known study.

Victor was looking finely. He had gained strength and manliness under his late experiences, and had made a very good soldier. He had come to stay "*one week*," he said, "then his furlough would be over." Victor enjoyed the quiet, lounging life, the comfortable fare and ease of his grand-father's house greatly. He said it was worth being deprived of ordinary comforts to enjoy them after-wards. "He had not been comfortable or seen a pretty woman for years." He asked after Panola. "She was well," Mark said, "but her mother was failing fast. The stiffness was spreading. It had seemed to stop for a long time, and then quite re-cently it had come on again." Victor said he would ride over in a day or so and see the Flanoys.

"Cherokee Joe was still there," Mark said, in reply to Victor's question. "His family also were living in a wigwam, built out in the bit of copse wood on the Flanoy estate. His wife made baskets and sewed and washed for Mrs. Flanoy, whose white servants had all left her. Panola does almost everything with her own hands," said Mark; "ex-cept for the little aid she gets from Joe's wife, and some little from Joe himself, she does *every thing*. But Mrs. Flanoy does not feel the change; Panola keeps her perfectly comfortable."

Mark went on to tell Victor that Panola not only took care of her mother, but that she also found time to see after himself and his grandfather, and to help her aunt Bolling. "Panola has her sewing-machine," Mark said, "and she made all sorts of clothing and little comfortable articles for all three households. She has entirely overcome her Indian dislike of manual labor. Her little hands are getting hardened from unaccustomed work."

"Have you heard from Natika lately?" asked Mark, his thoughts making contrast of the position of the two women.

"Yes," replied Victor, gloomily, "she broke off with the marchese. I knew she would."

"Where is she?" asked Mark.

"In Paris, very comfortable and happy," said Victor, bitterly. "Natika does not care for country or kinship, you know; that is, unless she should be attracted by the mere excitement of the thing to feel a transient impulse of patriotism. Natika might like to play Joan d'Arc for the interest of the character for a while. She would as lief run the blockade for the fun of the risk or the danger as not. I shouldn't be surprised to hear that she *had* tried it!" and Victor laughed. "I tell you what, Mark, I have learned one lesson in this miserable war, and that is the value of a true, single-hearted woman— such as Panola, for instance—who can sacrifice all her own desires and even comforts for the sake of those she loves. I have lost all fancy for useless queens of society."

Mark smiled. "You don't know yourself, Victor. Wait until you get back into the old grooves of life, and you will see then that habit is deep as life and strong as death. You will gradually go back to your old likings."

"No, I am sure not," replied Victor, energetically.

Victor went over to see the Flanoys that very evening. He went again the next day, and the next, and so he got to passing the greater portion of his days there. Panola struck him as being more beautiful than ever. Chicora had not changed at all. She welcomed him as kindly as formerly. Victor had known the rough life of a soldier. He appreciated the delightful atmosphere of home which surrounded these charming women, and which was lacking at his grandfather's. His attentions to Panola became more and more lover-like. Chicora was pleased to see this. Panola's future often was a heavy care to the afflicted mother. There was no one to look after Panola but the chief Satana, or Madame Bolling, in case of the mother's death. She believed Panola would not be happy living in the Nation, and towards Madame Bolling she cherished an instinctive hatred. She looked upon Victor's wooing, therefore, most favorably, and was resolved to use her influence to its utmost maternal limits in his favor.

But Panola grew shyer and colder as Victor grew warmer in his manner. When her mother would speak of him she was silent. She had been brought up in the habit of implicit obedience, and she knew it would be a hard trial for her to resist her afflicted but imperious mother's will, especially as she had no good reason for rejecting Victor. She liked him personally better than any one she knew, except—perhaps, Mark. Mark was out of the question. Not only was it impossible for him to think of love or marriage, but, even if it were possible, he had shown no feeling to justify Panola in thinking about him except as a dear brother.

Panola was a proud, shy, slowly-maturing, half Indian maiden. The chastity and continence of her blood through long lines of famous warriors had kept cool and as yet unwarmed by passion. She did not love any one so far as she knew, but neither did she desire to love. She did not wish to marry at all. She was happiest ministering to her mother, and to old Docteur Canonge, and to Mark, and in playing on her Straduarius. If she could have fled away into the vast depths of the forest, she would have done it to escape the importunities of Victor, and the imploring looks and entreaties of her mother on this disagreeable subject. Several times she thought she would appeal to Docteur Canonge or to Mark, to deliver her from what she felt to be a persecution. Once she got almost to the house, and to Mark's study, for this very purpose, when some strange impulse seemed to stay her feet, and she turned away and fled swiftly homeward, with crimson cheeks, like a frightened doe to its covert. Mark was so entirely convinced of Victor's devotion to Natika that he suspected nothing. Matters had gone on thus for the whole period of Victor's furlough. He was to leave on the following day, when he burst into Mark's study one hour before twilight, exclaiming:

"Congratulate me, Mark! for I am a bridegroom! I shall marry Panola to-morrow morning, just before I leave for the army. She has yielded at last."

Mark's book fell from his hands: the blow astounded him; he could not speak; the blood ebbed from his lips; he felt as if he was suffocating.

Victor was so much excited, and so gay over his triumph, that he did not observe the effect of his announcement upon his cousin. Mark rallied himself, stooped over to pick up his book, saying, in rather a smothered tone,

"You are certainly to be congratulated if this is true. When did it occur? How can you give up Natika?"

Victor's face fell.

"Natika has given me up," he said, sharply. "As for Panola, I have been intending to marry her, if I could, ever since I was here while you went to the Arkansas springs, and hard enough it has been to get her."

"I fear it was the difficulty that has been the

attraction," said Mark, sadly. "Do you *really* love Panola?"

"Yes; I think I do," said Victor, determinately setting his teeth together.

"Does Panola love you?" continued Mark, firmly.

"If she don't now, she *will*," replied Victor, almost angrily. Mark's questioning and doubts annoyed him. He was not so sure on any of the points as he would have liked to be. "She is not like most girls, Panola is not. She is naturally cold and unimpressionable; but she is very beautiful and good!"

"Oh, Victor!" said Mark, passionately, "don't force this poor girl to marry unless you are sure of yourself and of her. I fear you and her mother are acting cruelly to Panola. I know Mrs. Flanoy's imperious will. Panola is *not* cold; I have studied her nature, and I know it."

Victor was startled for the moment by the intense passion in Mark's voice. A suspicion flashed through his soul.

"*You* can't marry, Mark! I could not suspect you of the dog-in-the-manger desire to keep this girl single when you can offer her nothing but cold friendship!"

"God forbid!" said Mark, humbly. "I only desire Panola's happiness. I have never hoped for anything myself. But don't fetter her if she does not really love you : think a little of her wretchedness if she finds herself bound to a man who does not love her—whom she does not love."

"I am no Caliban or Bluebeard, Mark," said Victor, trying to smile, "and it is no use talking now, I shall marry Panola to-morrow. I have spoken to the magistrate to meet me at ten o'clock ; and immediately after the ceremony, which is only to be performed in order to satisfy Mrs. Flanoy, I go off to the army. I shall try for another furlough, when I will return to the bosom of my family," said he, with some return of his old levity of speech. He added more seriously, "Don't fear, Mark; I will not be unkind to my wife ! "

Mark sat with his face buried in his hands. He made no reply. Victor, vexed at his obstinate silence, left the room singing "Dites lui," from Offenbach's Grande Duchesse. He went to carry his great piece of news to his grandfather, who entered into his hopes with full sympathy and great excitement, which consoled Victor for Mark's coldness.

That was a night of agony for Mark, and his face bore the traces of it when he appeared at the breakfast table the next morning. He looked so pale and so ill that Docteur Canonge was seriously anxious ; and Victor did not require any further explanation as to the impossibility of Mark's going with the party to witness the brief ceremony to take place at

Mrs. Flanoy's. Victor dressed himself carefully in his gray uniform. He knew he would have but little time for change after the marriage. He was compelled to hasten in order to get to his command as soon as possible, as his furlough had expired.

Panola scarcely knew how she became engaged to Victor, or how it was that all the arrangements were made for her marriage. She had been impelled imperceptibly, step by step, by the force of her mother's will and Victor's importunities. She did not comprehend it, but she felt utterly helpless. If they would only let her alone; but that they would not do.

It was with a listless and indifferent hand that she clasped around her the fine white gown her mother had ordered her to wear as a wedding-gown. It was a pretty gown of fine India muslin, and Panola recollected that Mark had admired it greatly when she had worn it in his presence. She paused in the midst of her toilette to lean her head upon her hands and to sigh deeply. She did not weep—Panola was part Indian. She could have been burnt by a slow fire and still kept an imperturbable countenance. But there was on her face an expression of stolid endurance and stoical apathy which, however natural to it, had never been there before to-day.

The moments passed swiftly. Panola heard the driving up of the carriages which brought Docteur

Canonge and the magistrate, and she heard the gal-
loping of Victor's horse's feet as he dashed impatiently to the door. She looked out. Docteur
Canonge and the magistrate had just got out of
the carriages, which were being driven off to one
side. Mark was not with them; Panola thanked
God he had not come. She had dreaded his coming to
witness this dreadful marriage. Something had prevented his coming. Panola was glad. A low knock
at her door was answered by Panola's opening it.
Madame Bolling entered, smiling tenderly as she
held out a crown of lovely orange blossoms, fresh
from her garden. She embraced her niece with
effusion.

"Dear child," she said, "it is better I should not
be present at the ceremony. It would be painful to
me, and also to your mother. So I have brought
my small offering here. Wear my crown, Panola, in
this hour of your happiness. I had once fondly
hoped for different issues; but it is all ended. I
have also given to Joe's wife a handsome bride's
cake, which you will eat for my sake."

Madame Bolling kissed Panola affectionately,
arranged the crown upon her head, and then glided
noiselessly out of the room, and out of the house.

Panola was summoned; she obeyed; and somehow, she hardly knew how, she was in the salon
before the magistrate; and after a few words which
she scarcely heard—certainly did not *comprehend*—

she found herself in Victor's arms and he saluted her as "his wife." Then Docteur Canonge kissed her and blessed her, and cried over her, he was so pleased; and her mother smiled upon her with beautiful pleased eyes; and the handsome cake was cut and wine was drunk; then Victor embraced her again. He had drawn Panola to the door, talking to her with his arm about her waist; and there, with much tenderness, he had kissed her lips and her cheeks and then he was gone. Panola stood looking after him as he rode swiftly away. At the gate he paused and, turning, he waved his hand, and slowly lifting his hat, he sat bareheaded for an instant; then he disappeared from her view, riding rapidly away.

It was like a fearful dream! Panola felt so tired and so drowsy, somehow so stupefied. Instinctively she put up her hands, and took off the heavy wreath of orange flowers, with their overpowering scent. "I *do dislike* orange flowers," she thought, and that was really the only connected, conscious thought Panola had experienced that morning.

Victor, as he rode away, thought that he had never experienced a more painful chill than he had felt when he touched Panola's lips and cheeks, they were so icy cold. There were no bridal blushes there; but she was white as the cotton after which she was named. "She was like a woman made of marble," he thought; "I don't much like playing the part of a modern Pygmalion."

"What a strong smell of musk there is!" said Mrs. Flanoy to Panola. "It seems to be in your hair. It is very stupefying!"

"It must have come from the strong perfume of my orange-flower crown," said Panola. "They are so powerful, indoors, you know. I do not like them in masses."

CHAPTER XX.

PASSING AWAY.

THINGS settled down into their accustomed quiet in this little nook, while great events were occurring all around, and the fate of nations was being decided. Mrs. Flanoy was growing weaker and weaker, but the flame of life burned more fiercely and high, the nearer it came to its extinction. It seemed to condense itself more and more into her eyes, which were at once fearful and most beautiful to look into. There is a picture at Pompeii which is brought to mind by the remembrance of Chicora's face. It is a mosaic, which has retained all its brilliancy of coloring and freshness of hue for over a thousand years. It represents a head severed from the body, but without any painful accompaniments. The head is placed upright upon a square slab of marble. From beneath this marble there is slowly flowing a stream of crimson blood, in which a black vulture, seated near by, is dipping his savage beak. There is no contortion of muscle in the living decapitated head. The beautiful features are quiet and fixed; the eyes are wide open, and look straight forward, defying fate and death, and time, and Nemesis. Dark and bright they gaze in utter contempt of the vulture feeding to satiety on the life-blood. They do not even see the vulture. They look steadfastly on into a higher and eternal life, seeking to meet its equals among the gods. So Chicora looked.

After a time, Panola had quietly resumed her usual ministrations to the three families so dependent upon her. When she drew near to the well-known study in which Mark was sitting as usual, she felt a sudden faintness come over her. She sat down on a bench on the verandah, outside of the door, and gasped for breath; but it was soon over—that passing spasm. She rose, and, turning the knob of the door quietly, she entered the room. Mark looked up and the color rushed over his face. "Panola," he ejaculated.

"Yes, Mark," said Panola, with a plaintive sadness in her voice, which was quite firm; and she gave him her hand as usual. Mark's fingers closed over it involuntarily; then he recollected himself and let it drop. It had rested in his very tranquilly, as cold as a small snowflake. Panola began to busy herself about the house, just as usual.

Mark could scarcely fix his eyes or his mind upon the book he held between his trembling fingers. He found himself straining his ears to catch the sound of her light footsteps as she moved about the cottage "putting things to rights," as women say. Then she brought in a lot of clothing that needed mending.

"I'll take these home and do them, Mark," she said. "I can't leave mamma very long."

Panola was very quiet and grave in her manner. Mark saw a great change had come over the young girl: somehow the splendor of the sheen of her beauty had departed; there was no color at all in her cheeks. Her face was all satiny white except her lips; they seemed to be burning with fever-red. The glory, too, had faded, somehow, out of her hair. She looked, again, like the pale white child that Mark remembered so well, and that Victor had laughed at so much. The life seemed gradually dying out of her as the splendid hues of a wounded butterfly do in its prolonged death-agony. But the faculty of endurance, proud and high, was stamped upon her every feature. She would die and make no sign, as so many of her race had done before her in the earlier ages—as her mother was perishing now, day by day, before her eyes. She had no vain cries or lamentations to make against any fate. She was not of the softer mould of the pure white race or of the childish African. She knew how to suffer and to be still.

12

Mark looked after her as she disappeared through the door with the basket of clothes in her hand, and a deep, prolonged sigh told what he was feeling; but he picked up his book, and again set himself resolutely to his study. He repeated to himself in a low voice a sonnet of Anne C. Lynch, one of her finest:

"Go forth in life, oh friend! not seeking love;
A mendicant, that with imploring eye
And outstretched hand asks of the passers-by
The alms his strong necessities may move.
For such poor love, to pity near allied,
Thy generous spirit may not stoop and wait,
A suppliant whose prayer may be denied
Like a spurned beggar's at a palace gate:
But thy heart's affluence lavish uncontrolled:
The largess of thy love give full and free
As monarchs in their progress scatter gold;
And be thy heart like the exhaustless sea
That must its wealth of cloud and dew bestow,
Through tributary streams or ebb or flow."

There is much value in the acquired power which all true culture gives of self-control, at least of external self-control. It is a duty that every one owes to humanity to keep out of sight of others mental or physical pain. The intuitive chord of sympathy which binds man to man should be respected and never made to jar or quiver unnecessarily. One has *no right* to exploiter one's selfish griefs or discomforts. A decent respect for others should forbid this. It is not hypocrisy, but a rightful considera-

tion for others which makes the dwellers in the
Hall of Eblis in Vathek cover with their right
hands the dark hole in their breasts in which their
hearts are ever burning. People are so much affected
by their surroundings, what right has one to shadow
over the horizon of others? The truly magnanimous
soul, who loves his fellows, may seek sympathy in
joy, but must keep sorrow to itself. Panola nor
Mark either asked for sympathy from any one.
What was to be endured they bore in silence and
with outward calm. They had no pity for weakness in themselves, but great charity for others, and
—they were hopeless—they had never had any hope.
It is human to submit with patience to the inevi-
table. One gathers up the fragments into the
baskets, grateful for even the crumbs that are left
from the feasts of others' lives.

CHAPTER XXI.

CHICORA'S DEATH.

TIME passed. The Confederacy was ended;
Lee had surrendered; the army was paroled,
and yet Victor had not returned to his family—to
his bride of an hour. His letters had been frequent

and all that was tender for months. Suddenly they ceased to arrive. Chicora fretted over this sudden silence more than Panola. Docteur Canonge was open in his wonder and his denunciation of the cruel circumstances which were keeping Victor away so long. Mark feared in silence. Panola said nothing. "He will come when he is ready," she would say to her impatient mother.

A friend on business called to see Mark. He had just come from New Orleans. He mentioned seeing Victor, and also Natika, who was summoned there by her agents about her affairs. Mark turned pale. "Natika in America! Natika in New Orleans!" Alas! for Victor! What humiliation lay in store for Panola! Mark trembled.

The visitor had scarcely quitted Mark before the door of his room opened and Panola stood before him. Her face was flushed and her eyes were dilated, whether with grief or joy it was impossible to say. She held a letter in her outstretched hand to Mark.

"Mark!" she said, breathlessly, "Mark! I have come to you! See!—read! Victor has deserted me! Oh! Mark!"

The tension of feeling was too great. She sunk in a dead faint at Mark's feet. He cried aloud for aid. He dragged himself from his chair and lifted her head from the floor. Lizbette came running in; she brought water and soon restored Panola to consciousness. Panola pushed the hair back which had fallen from the confining ribbons, rubbed her eyes and looked around in a confused state of mind. But her eyes grew intelligent as she saw Mark sitting by her on the floor, and the letter lying where it had dropped from her hand as she fell. Lizbette had trodden it under foot. Panola stretched out her hand to reach it.

"I remember now," she said. "It is Victor's letter! Read it! He is gone to Natika! He will never come back again! He is gone forever! Read it!"

Mark snatched the letter from her, read it, and every vein on his forehead swelled with indignation as he did read it. Victor wrote desperately. He threw himself upon Panola's generosity for forgiveness of all the wrong and humiliation he was doing her. He said that he could make no reparation but to leave her. He had again met the only woman he had ever really loved, and he was now separated from her as well as from Panola by his own mad act; his future must be miserable, he said, but he would spend it alone, far from both. At last he had found that Natika loved him; he did not think Panola would suffer as much as *she* had, or as *he* did; if she could find any redress at the law, he thought she had better seek it. Then he begged her to forgive him, and to pity his utter misery in being compelled to write such words to her; he would never look on her face again.

Mark angrily flung the letter from him.

"Dastardly villain!" he said, "with no purpose nor strength—unstable as water; a curse to himself and to all connected with him."

Panola laid her hand lightly on Mark's arm.

"Mark," she said, "don't blame poor Victor so much. It is better so! better so! I did not love Victor as I should have done! The thing now is to give him freedom and to tell mamma. Oh! Mark, how *shall* I tell this to mamma? she is so devoted to Victor," and Panola began to weep for the first time in all her troubles; the tears streamed forth freely; she leaned her head on the arm of Mark's chair and sobbed aloud.

Mark moved his hand as if to lay it soothingly upon the bowed, light head, but checked himself and leaned back with a fixed look in his face. He clasped his hands tightly together so they should not be tempted to stray lovingly over her head, and he sat trembling like a leaf. Panola wept on—oh! the blessed relief of those tears.

"Who was to tell Docteur Canonge?" Mark thought, and shrank from the task.

The dear, fond old man! Every feeling would be outraged by Victor's base conduct. His keen sense of honor, his pride, his affection, all wounded to the very quick. Mark groaned aloud.

He agreed with Panola that great caution would be requisite in breaking this news to Mrs. Flanoy.

He was willing to undertake the painful duty as soon as he had explained all to his grandfather. So Panola rose up, dried her eyes and went home, in order to send Cherokee Joe with some vehicle in which Mark might be conveyed to Mrs. Flanoy's. Mark was in the habit of riding out in a carriage when they had been able to keep up an equipage. Poor Confederates now had neither horses nor carriages.

Mark had a sorrowful scene with his grandfather. The old man tore his hair when he had read Victor's letter; he raved; he wept; his affliction was dreadful to see. His pity for Panola was infinite, and yet he said "it was better she should be freed from such a base, dishonorable man as Victor." Mark soothed the fiery, high-spirited old man as well as he could, and at last got off so as to go to Mrs. Flanoy's in the chair which Cherokee Joe had by this time brought to the door.

Mark felt himself quail for a few moments before his painful task. He rolled himself along the level galleries, and into the room where Chicora was lying, unsuspicious of the heart-rending information he was conveying to her. Chicora greeted Mark very affectionately. Molly, the wife of Joe, was sitting by Chicora.

"I am really glad you happened to come to see me, Mark," said Chicora. "I was thinking of sending after Docteur Canonge. My heart seems to be very queer to-day. It beats so irregularly, and sometimes seems to pause for a whole second in its pulsation. I fear the stiffness is spreading internally. Have you heard anything yet from Victor? I do wish he was here! Why don't he come?"

Mark drew a long breath and nerved himself, then as gently and tenderly as he could he told the sad tale of his cousin's unpardonable abandonment of Panola to the amazed and even incredulous woman. As his full meaning burst upon her mind, a cry escaped her lips; a shrill, fierce cry, like the scream of an angry eagle. It harrowed Mark's very soul. After that one cry Chicora lay silent for a moment, then, turning her eyes towards the Indian Molly, she uttered a few words in the Cherokee tongue. Molly threw up her hands over her head in a passionate, savage gesture, and quitted the room.

In a few moments the door opened noiselessly and Cherokee Joe stood motionless before Chicora's couch. She looked at him, her eyes pouring out red, fiery light; her voice was low and monotonous as she spoke in her native tongue. She hissed the sentences out slowly and emphatically. Joe started at Chicora's first words, and cast an angry look at Mark, then his face grew stolid and fixed as he listened to Chicora. His wife had stolen back, and at Chicora's last words she held out to Joe one of the diamond snakes, the totem which Panola usually wore. Joe lifted the snake high above his head and said some words in the Cherokee, which his wife solemnly repeated after him. Mark only distinguished the words "Satana" and "Panola." He saw from the pantomime an oath was being registered on the totem. Joe thrust the snake into his bosom and glided out of the room. Chicora smiled, a fearful smile of anticipated vengeance, as she looked after Joe's retreating figure, then she closed her eyes with a long, shuddering sigh. A faint, weary look came over her face. "Mark," she whispered, "my heart flutters."

Mark put his fingers upon her temple to count the throbbings. His face turned white: the pulsation was nearly gone.

"I must have grandfather here," he said quickly to Molly. "Send for him instantly."

Chicora smiled; she revived; she said, "It is all over; my hour is come; call Panola; you will be good to my child, Mark, if possible; you will do whatever you can; you are good and true— send for Panola."

She came running swiftly. She hastened to her mother; bent over her in anguish: "Mamma! my mother! my darling!"

Chicora fixed her eyes on her child: "My child," she said, gently, "my poor, lonely daughter! the Great Spirit calls for me; even now the angel of

death pauses upon my threshold. He is welcome!
Let the messenger of the All-father enter in peace!
Chicora is very weary; her heart has been bleeding
long, and she longs for rest. You will be strong
to bear all that comes to you; you will not weep for
Victor. A Cherokee does not weep. Joe will go
to Satana. The chief will look after you. The
white man is not good to be trusted; and now, my
child, good-bye; Chicora goes to the Great Father."
Panola kissed her mother in silent anguish.

Chicora had closed her eyes calmly after speaking
to her daughter. She whispered now: "Let me
pass in peace; there should be no tears nor outcry
at the deathbed of Chicora; she is the daughter of
chiefs. I forbid you to weep."

Panola uttered a great sob, then with an immense
effort of will she controlled her natural grief, and
kneeling down by her mother laid her arm over
her, fixed her eyes steadily upon her face and was
quiet and moveless as stone. Chicora lay calm and
smiling. Her breathing grew slower and slower;
slight convulsions passed over her face. The great
struggles of her heart could be counted in the
intense silence. From time to time Chicora would
open her eyes and look steadily into the eyes of her
child. There seemed to be an interchange of nerve-
aura between the two: at that supreme moment
they were conscious of the oneness of their spirits.
Mark sat perfectly immovable, looking in awe at

the two women whose souls were so strong in the bitterest sorrows of humanity.

Suddenly Chicora spoke a few words to Molly in the native tongue. The woman rose to her feet, and standing erect at the foot of Chicora's couch, she began to sing a low, solemn chant, the death-song of Chicora. The woman's voice was very sweet and clear, and Mark could follow the changes of meaning from the cadences, now plaintive and soft, now triumphant and joyous, as she chanted the youth, the beauty, the happiness of Chicora, and then the sorrows of her chequered life.

Chicora's expressive countenance changed according to the words of the song. Molly's voice sunk to a soft wail as she uttered the prayers for peace and rest that the dying woman craved. A beautiful serenity spread over her features, and as the song died away consciousness faded out of her eyes. Chicora never spoke again. Docteur Canonge came, but could do nothing for her. That night she died.

"It is the strangest malady I ever saw," said Docteur Canonge; "I have seen nothing like it in all my practice."

CHAPTER XXII.

THE PHILOSOPHY OF LOVE.

MARK wrote briefly and sternly to Victor, telling him of the resolution of Panola to seek a divorce from the bonds which fettered both; and of the death of Chicora. He received several wildly agitated, almost incoherent letters in response, from which he gathered an idea of the condition of mind in which his half-frantic cousin now was living.

Natika had heard in Paris of Victor's marriage. Her first feeling was that of indignant rage at the unexpected escape of the slave, who had given to her his life-long homage. Her second impulse was that she would break up all these impertinent arrangements, and therefore she sailed for America. Besides, she was not well; she had had a very exhausting season; she had been very gay and had latterly felt as if the pursuit of vapid amusements was a great labor. She was thoroughly out of health, and also out of temper. Her physicians prescribed rest and a sea-voyage; so she came home.

On arriving in New Orleans, she ascertained Victor's whereabouts, and she wrote a few hasty lines to him, making no allusion whatever to his marriage, as if she had never heard of it. Victor hesitated about meeting her. He took up his pen to write her to tell her of his marriage; but then a great desire came over him to see her for himself, and to tell her of it himself. And this feeling was not unmixed with a sensation of bitter curiosity to see how Natika would receive the news of his emancipation from her power. In an evil moment Victor yielded to this impulse, and instead of writing to Natika, went to her. He found her looking badly, pale and thin. She met him with unusual tenderness, and he felt his soul faint within him as he received her affectionate greeting, and thought of what he had to communicate to her. But it had to be done.

Victor stammered out his tale like a culprit. Natika heard it with open scorn and anger—Victor hoped even with some jealousy. She snatched her hand from his after he had made his confession, and with a few bitter, scathing words, she dragged her skirts away from contact with him as he was sitting beside her. Then she burst into tears and quitted the room in a whirlwind of passion and temper. For the first time in his life Victor thought that Natika loved him, and though the first sensation of this made his heart leap as it never had before, yet the next moment, when he recollected the barriers he had placed between Natika and himself, the very blood seemed to freeze in his veins. He became icy cold. An immense wave of hatred towards Panola, and himself too, surged through him.

He staggered out of the room and got somehow into his own apartment. He threw himself down in a chair with a groan of utter desperation. He felt half dead and utterly bewildered. He sat so for hours, then, with the strength of despair, he wrote his wild letter to Panola, and one equally wild to Natika; and resolved to put an end to it all, and to himself too. But Natika knew him. He had scarcely closed and sealed his last letter to her, and he had the pistol in his hand to make a finish of all things, when Natika rapped violently at his door. Receiving no response, she forced it open; the key had not caught firmly when he had attempted to lock it with his agitated hand. Natika sprang in and seized the pistol from Victor.

"I knew it!" she exclaimed. "Oh, Victor, what a craven you are! Too weak to live, and yet you would condemn me to eternal misery and infinite remorse by your own folly and madness."

He did not reply. He looked gloomily at Natika.

"What else is left?" he asked.

She saw that he was desperate. She came to him. She put her arms around his neck. She laid her head upon his bosom. Victor embraced her passionately.

"Victor," she said, "you have placed barriers between us that I can not pass. But one thing I can do, and that I will do. I can not give myself to you, but I can *live* for you, and keep myself free from any other ties for your sake; that I will do."

Victor threw himself at her feet and buried his head in the hem of her garment; and he wept bitterly.

"Natika," he sobbed, "Natika, show me how to give my life to you. You know it has always been yours."

So Natika triumphed, but she continued to play the role of an almost broken-hearted woman, her paleness and emaciation aiding in keeping up the character satisfactorily.

Natika was half deceived herself; she was such a good actress, for the moment she entered so entirely into any impersonation, that she was, pour le moment, that creature of the imagination, whether it was Hermione or Camille, or, as now, a sentimental, much-injured, sensitive woman. And Victor believed in her, and he was so flattered by this late acknowledged love of Natika's. And he *knew* Panola did not love him! He cursed his fate and his own obstinacy thousands of times; and he eagerly sought the consolation of Natika's tenderness. He felt somehow as if a bond, perhaps of lonely guiltiness, united them the closer. In all mankind he and Natika were alone, even in the general condemnation and social reproach that he knew would follow both. Though Natika had too much self-respect and too much wisdom to give herself wholly to him, yet there was a delirious sort of rapture for Victor in merely beholding her and knowing that she never would belong to another.

Very few men or women are really capable of the highest sentiment of love. The majority of both sexes are impelled toward each other by mere instincts, which, of course, are valuable as any other instincts, and quite as necessary as any other impulses to make a perfect man or woman. Human nature is defective without *all* the passions, but the ordinary impulses must be controlled by education and culture and right reason in order to make a fine human being.

The electric forces which draw man and woman to each other, the general and ordinary magnetism, which may be only *physical*, or perhaps more justly be called *chemical*, the affinity which unites atom to atom in all physical nature, which is often experienced in life among human beings, in a stronger or weaker degree, is *not* the truest and highest sentiment which the human soul is capable of feeling. And the reason why there are so many wretched marriages is because men and women mistake this common and universal magnetism, for *real preference*, for true sympathy, for holiest love; and it fails them, as all mere physical impulses do; as hunger does when it is satisfied. Most people love "*love*," not the individual *lover*. They like soft tones and tender words and warmth of embraces. But of the absolute oneness of soul and sympathy, the inexhaustible fountain of true fellowship, and eternal progression together in love and excellence towards the highest—*that* few do know, or few pause to think about. Yet this is the only satisfying love; and it is *possible!* When a soul is so happy as to attain to this love, life is enriched and glorified beyond ordinary conception. Even if the love should never be what is called fortunate—that is, if the two, loving in this holy manner, should never belong to one another—there remains the exquisite bliss of having been once fully comprehended; of being *perfectly* appreciated and *understood.* And the parted ones are better and nobler and happier. Their souls can never be utterly lonely. If deprived of the ordinary joys of life, they have the highest and purest still left—a conscious sympathy in progressing towards the goal of the highest possible for humanity.

There is nothing so fearful to man as utter loneliness and isolation from all sympathy. It is a sorrowful fate to be alone; and those men and women who wreck their natures under the leading of lower impulses, miss the deepest joy of life.

Mark, even in his wretchedest hours, felt this. His love for Panola was a distinguishing preference. Out of all the earth she was the *one* elected woman for him. She, too, was capable of such a love. Natika was not; and he pitied Victor and Natika

13

more than he did himself or Panola, as these thoughts rushed often through his mind.

Docteur Canonge was so much grieved by the conduct of Victor and Natika, that he never spoke of them but once to Mark after he heard of their hasty marriage. Then he said, quietly:

"It is exceeding great misfortune for boz of zem, and for zeir offspring. Zey have neider of zem good constitution. Victor have de mos' feeble of zie two. I can foresee no good result from zis marriage. I sink, wiz Plato, zat a government—zat is, society— has zie right to forbid such marriages as will entail upon humanity weak and imperfect generation of men and women. In zat I disagree wiz George Sand, and George Eliot, too. George Sand teaches in her novels, wiz her powerful pen, zat zie height of human love is zie imitation of zie Divine love of Christ, and zerefore zie highest love is zat of entire self-abnegation or charitee, in which zie woman sall love her inferior, from whom she can expect nozing, and who will probably repay her devotion wiz ingratitude. So she teaches in 'Lucrezia Floriani,' and ordinarily also in all zat she writes. Her heroes are usually poor sticks. And also George Eliot, she make her women always zie nobler of zie two, like Maggie in 'Zie Mill on zie Floss,' and 'Romola,' and also in her ozer books. Zat is not good instruction for young people. Zie trutt is, zat whatever we cherish as our ideal will generally form our character. What we love, we will grow like. Zat is a rule in physics, and also metaphysics. All zie young peoples should be taught zie lessons of psychology and of physiology; and zey should learn to govern zeir impulses wiz right reason. Zey should be instructed zat zey owe someting to humanity, and zat zey must often make great sacrifice for zie good of zie race. Zere can be no compensation to humanity for an imperfect child, and zerefore marriage zould be in some degree a matter of legislation of zie State. Plato is right. Zie charitee or love of Christ, which zie modern writers do hold up for imitation, is good in zie dominion of external brotherhood only. It is not intended to govern, except generally; not zie world of inner life and reproduction of kind. Zie man or zie woman who love, as zeir highest, imperfect and undeveloped beings, lower zan zeirselves, cider physically or morally or mentally, zey show a blunted moral sense. One can pity an inferior, but not love zem wiz zie highest of zie soul-gifts. And it is great wrong to humanity. Of course I do not speak of zie accidents of life—rank, birth or wealth. I do not regard zem. I mean zie personality of zie two. No one should ever marry wizout fullest love and fullest health, both of mind and body. And when zose qualities are found, zen people should marry as a duty to society, wezer zey be rich or poor. Sympathy and health, zat is essential, and this should be legislated upon."

"What an old Platonist he is," thought Mark. "And so sweet and good, too."

CHAPTER XXIII.

MADAME BOLLING'S FLOWERS.

MARK was sitting in his chair. He had rolled himself out of the room in which Chicora's body lay. The coffin which was to receive it had to come from a distance, and Mark had undertaken the night watch with Indian Joe, by the body. The two men sat silently hour by hour. The room in which Chicora lay was brilliantly lighted, but the adjoining apartment in which Mark and Joe now sat was dark. The door was open between the chambers, and Mark had a clear view of the couch upon which the remains were lying, covered over with a white sheet. Some flowers were scattered upon it. Joe sat with his head bent down, his hands clasped around his knees, as he crouched on the floor by Mark in the attitude of Indian mourning. He had sat motionless as a fakir all the night.

It was now past midnight. Mark was meditating on all the past, lost in his recollections, when suddenly he felt in the darkness the pressure of Joe's hand upon his, and a smothered "hist" from the Indian's lips. The door entering from the verandah into the next room slowly opened, a figure clothed in deep black glided in, followed by the bent form of old Nana. The old negress tottered in, shaking her white head as if it was palsied, keeping as close as she could to her mistress, for it was indeed Madame Bolling, who came in now unbidden and unchecked into the presence of the dead woman who had so hated her. Madame was dressed in deep mourning, and had a black hood drawn over her head. The hem of her skirts was wet and draggled with the heavy night-dews she had walked through in coming from the Pavilion to the house.

Madame looked around, but seeing no one, she came forward into the room. She stood by the corpse. Mark felt Cherokee Joe's hand closing over his with the clasp of an iron vice. The two men watched. Madame Bolling laid the sheet back from the proud, sad, silent face. It was very noble in its sculptured stillness. Madame looked down upon it steadfastly. Nana crept up by her side, and looked too. Madame gazed until she was satisfied, then taking some flowers out from under her cloak, she placed them on the breast of the corpse. "I bring my offering, Chicora," she said, in a low voice. "You hated me and you are *here*," laying the sheet back over the dead face.

Madame Bolling went out as quietly as she had entered the room. Nana hobbled after her. Releasing Mark's hand, Joe went swiftly to the side of the body. Mark rolled himself after him. The wheels of Mark's chair were noiseless. They were kept covered with felt to prevent noise. Joe had taken out the flowers that Madame Bolling had placed on Chicora's breast. They were a pretty bunch of sweet pea blossoms, tied with a white satin riband. Joe looked at them, smelled them, and handed them to Mark. Mark did the same. They were harmless flowers enough. Joe took the flowers as Mark laid them down on the sheet again, and going to the window he threw them out as far as he could send them.

"Chicora not like Madame Bolling," he said to Mark. "Not like her flowers."

Mark nodded his head. He thought Joe was right.

CHAPTER XXIV.

A SUCCESSFUL DEBUTANTE.

THE Southern States were in a very prostrate condition. All property was greatly depressed in value. Taxes were in arrears, and the labor was so uncertain that those who had most land were the worst off. They had more taxes and debts to pay, and less money to meet their obligations with. The sugar estates were lying fallow for hundreds of miles, and the people who owned them were absolutely starving in the midst of their fertile but uncultivated fields. Little debts accumulated from interest, and large plantations were sold for a mere trifle. The people were very poor and unaccustomed to labor. It was very piteous. The mere physical distress was agonizing to witness. Misery, wretchedness, and a feeble struggle for the bare necessaries of life met the eye on every side. The misfortune was universal. A whole race had gone down in this Titanic fight, and now they were perishing off the earth, which had no further use for that class of people. Nature appears to be very pitiless, but the roots of progress seem to be planted always in the grave of the past.

Three races were dying out now in the Southern States. There was the race of the white slave-owner, the aristocratic gentleman of America. His knell had been sounded. Then the fiat had gone forth against the red Indian. He was to be hunted from off the earth. Then the doom had been written on the wall against the African. He was to be absorbed and to be killed by vice and intemperance, and lack of moral discipline. None but the strong races can survive in this perpetual conflict of humanity. Its issues are good for the world, but individuals suffer in the trampling under foot of this mastodon, Progress.

Philosophers may watch with intelligent gaze this changing woof in the loom of earthly life. But often the threads may be dyed in the philosopher's heart's blood. It is only the gods who sit upon the height of Olympus who survey human affairs with calm eyes and impartial interest. Some clever people had foreseen the end of the strife, and had wisely made provision against the evil day.

Amongst these was Madame Bolling. She had managed somehow, by trading and "looking around," to pick up a few hundred bales of cotton, which she now sold at the price of four hundred dollars per bale. It gave her a nice little sum to start again in the world with.

Panola had left her place in her aunt's care, while she had gone to New Orleans to consult a lawyer as to the mode necessary for her to take in order to free Victor from the bonds he had put upon his

own hands as well as hers. She found little difficulty; though the laws of Louisiana are very
stringent in regard to marriage, yet the proof of
Victor's abandonment of his wife of an hour was
so conclusive, being his own statements in his own
letter, that the judge gave the decision immediately
in favor of the divorce, allowing Panola to resume
her maiden name of Flanoy.

While she was in New Orleans attending to this
business, she was astounded to see a notice in the
papers of the sale of her mother's property on account of a small debt and judgment for back taxes.
The sale was by the sheriff of the parish, and her
aunt had bought in the whole property for a mere
song. Panola had known nothing of the matter
until she saw this notice. But the next day she
had a letter from her aunt, telling her that she had
purchased the estate, and offering to Panola a home
with her in very affectionate terms.

Panola laid the letter down with surprise. She
did not understand this move at all. But it all
seemed to be done legally. She also had a letter
from Mark, reproaching her for not letting him
know about this debt and the condition of her
affairs. "He might, perhaps, have found some
means of aiding her, or at least of raising the money
by mortgage on the property."

Panola was amazed; but one thing was clear to
her. She had lost her estate. If she had known

of it in time, she was sure, if she had applied to
Satana, he would have helped her. But what to do
now she did not see. A home with her aunt Bolling she would not accept. Though Panola had
never shared her mother's dislike to her aunt, yet
she felt somehow as if she would not like to live
with or to be dependent on her. So she wrote a
note declining her aunt's proffered kindness; and to
Mark she wrote, frankly telling him she had not
known anything about the law suit and judgment.
But it was too late to remedy the evil now. The
property was gone. Docteur Canonge wrote a loving letter to Panola, inviting her to come "to take
care of him and his poor Mark." Panola wept
over the affectionate letter of the good old man.
But she could not go to Docteur Canonge. Shortly
afterward Mark received this letter from her:

"DEAR MARK:—I have at last succeeded in
arranging my little affairs. Through the kindness
of Von La Hache and Olivera, who aided me, the
one on the piano, and the other with his exquisite
violin, I gave a very successful concert here last
night. You will see the notice of it in the papers
of the day, which I send you. The laudations are
rather extravagant, but it was quite a little triumph
for me. I was rather not frightened, more *excited*,
when Olivera led me on to the stage, violin in hand.
(My Straduarius is finer than his instrument.)

You know mine was found in Mexico in an old Spanish family, where it had been an heirloom, and papa paid an immense sum for it. Poor papa! He little thought he was purchasing a means for his daughter to make her bread. At first, my eyes took in a sea of faces and heads that made my own head swim. But Von La Hache struck a bold chord to cover my confusion, and Olivera kindly whispering 'courage, allons,' drew his bow across the violin in the first notes of our duo, which it had been considered best for me to make my essay in public with. At the sound of the violin a wonderful sense of power stole over me, and settling my Straduarius, I drew my bow with as much firmness of touch and clearness of tone as I ever did in my life. I forgot the faces, and only listened to the witching notes from Olivera's instrument as it mounted, like a bird, higher and higher, I following in a vain emulation, until at last we both burst out into a gush of music that carried us both away. I believe we both forgot the audience. I am sure I did, until I was recalled to consciousness by the storm of applause. It was very exciting, the waving of handkerchiefs, and the air seemed to rain flowers, as bouquets fell all over the stage around us.

"After we had retired, during the interval, Von La Hache seized my hands in ecstacy. 'Dear Madame, your fortune is made. You play like an angel.'

"Well! You know *Francia's angels are* playing on violins in those famous pictures of his. And I have seen a St. Cecelia also playing on the violin. So Von La Hache's compliment was not so far out of the way. The issue of it all, dear Mark, is that your little Panola is become suddenly famous. The impressario of the opera house has called upon me this morning, with proposals for a series of concerts, and others have been here, editors and all sorts of people, urging different kinds of engagements and plans upon me until my head aches. But I think I shall accept an offer from an agent who wishes me to give concerts in all the principal cities, and perhaps I shall go to Europe. I have secured a good respectable maid, over middle age, to accompany me. Love to grandpapa Canonge and to Lizbette.   Your affectionate

"PANOLA.

"P. S.—I have made one thousand dollars already by my concerts. You see I shall be quite rich if I go on. Dear Mark, you must let me help grandpapa Canonge. I know how proud you are about money, but I have a right to help the dear old man, who is like my father. I shall deposit money from time to time, subject to your order, for *his use.* You can draw it without letting him know. Won't you do this for *me?*—for *Panola?*"

Mark read this letter with mingled feelings. He

was proud of Panola's great success, and yet he
disliked the publicity of it all.   He disliked to
take money from her, and yet he saw how it would
hurt her if he refused it.   They were very poor
now.   The old docteur was getting too old and too
feeble to continue his practice.   Lizbette was old
and rheumatic, and Mark was helpless.   His three
hundred per annum, from his uncle Jacob's will,
was really all that they had to depend upon to keep
the little household from destitution.   His grandfather talked of selling his books, but Mark knew
that that would break the old man's heart; and
then he would get little or nothing for them in the
depressed condition of the country.   Mark thought
over every thing.   Victor and Natika had both
written, proffering aid to their grandfather and to
Mark, but both had rejected it with scorn.   They
had disclaimed all further intercourse with Victor
and Natika, who had gone away together and had
been privately married as soon as Panola had pro-
cured the divorce.

Mark snatched a piece of paper, and wrote in
reply to Panola, congratulating her upon her success as a musicienne, and assuring her of the hearty
sympathy of his grandfather and himself in all her
undertakings.   In regard to the money, he said,
" Yes, Panola, I will take from *you* so much as is
needful for the comfort of my grandfather, who
loves you so much ; and even what *I* absolutely

need I will take from *you*—what I would not from any other living being. But I have enough for my small wants, you know, from my uncle Jacob's will. Write to us daily, Panola. We miss you every hour, and talk of you, and think of you always.

"Your friend and relative,

"MARK BOLLING."

Poor Mark wrote and rewrote and erased his letter in order to get it cool enough, and yet to give some expression to gratitude natural under the circumstances and proper to be expressed. So Panola started off on her tour of concert-giving, and she wrote a journal, which she sent back continually to the little household, which she called now "home." It was the only excitement they had in the quiet monotony of the sad country; and Mark looked with impatient eagerness for the daily coming of the long letters which never failed, and which amused grandfather Canonge excessively. Panola's observations were so original and so fresh. The old man would laugh till tears were in his eyes, over her descriptions of scenes and the people she met.

CHAPTER XXV

PANOLA'S letters and a visit from an occasional tourist, attracted by Docteur Canonge's scientific fame, were the chief events in life to Mark now, when suddenly one morning Professor Römer presented himself at the gate. He was travel-worn and weary, and did not look at all like a respectable individual, his habiliments being considerably the worse for wear. But he had bought himself a shiny tall beaver hat, and a new cloth overcoat, which he displayed to Mark with all the joy of a child.

Mark fairly embraced Römer, and Docteur Canonge rapturously kissed him on both cheeks. Römer was at home in a few seconds, and then, after resting a day, he proceeded to enjoy himself in his own fashion. He brought out his blotting books and tin boxes, and took possession of part of the library. He was gratified at the opportunity to study the unknown flora of this country. Cherokee Joe had made his appearance again, and had taken up his quarters at Docteur Canonge's. He wouldn't go to Madame Bolling's house, but he might be seen at any hour of the day lounging about with his gun on his shoulder, or bringing a brace of teal or snipe from "the ponds."

Lizbette was always willing to give Joe what she
called " his *wittles*," because he kept the larder supplied with game.   Joe slept in the hay-loft over
the stable at night; but he could be found in the
evenings sitting bolt upright at the kitchen fire,
gazing into the blaze, and breaking his obstinate
silence with the customary "ughs," in reply to
Lizbette, who was glad to have anybody to talk to,
even if it was only an Indian.

Professor Römer made friends with Joe, who
showed him where all the rarest and strangest
plants grew.   One morning the professor came into
Mark's study with his box of specimens well filled,
and Joe followed after him, bearing a game-bag
stuffed with the similar spoils of innocent science.
Joe stood and watched with great curiosity, while
the professor seated himself and began to arrange
and label his specimens for drying.   It amused
Mark too, and he aided the professor in laying the
plants straight between the sheets of blotting paper
which the professor carried about for this purpose.
The professor talked all the time in broken English.
He was a very communicative, genial man.

Joe had deposited his bag on the table, and stood
now by it, immovably upright, with his hand upon
his gun; his bright, black eyes glancing curiously
at Mark and the professor as they worked and
talked about the plants before them.

"This mornin'," said the professor, "I have had

great success. I saw growing outside in the road, near von leetle house mit verandah, quite ruinous now, a plant what I have never yet see in dis contree. It grow plentiful in Europe, and I know it dere well. I was sure it could not be natif here. It stray ver like out of die garten of die house, or out of some cultivated place. It was die plant dat I do know. I examine him well. He was quite leetle. But I know die leaf. So I tell Joe dat I like to go inside in dat leetle house place for to see if zere was ever a garten. Joe say 'ugh,' and we clime over die fence. Dere was no gate or it was nail up, and we get in dis leetle house garten. It was so vild. Every ting was vild. It have been long neglectit, but dere vas, oh, great variety of thos' interestin' plants dere dat I tink I ever see in one place togedder. Der was many natif plants, very interestin', and also dere was oders not natif. It was mos remarkable, die number of plants medicinal dere. I gader a great many. Some what you call die plants of poison. But so all is medicine. Medicine is poison, bad use; and poison is medicine, good use. I find dis leetle plant plenty in dere. Some of him was bloomin', here is he." And Professor Römer held up a spray of pea blossoms   Mark started. He recognized the flowers. They were of the same kind as those that Madame Bolling had laid upon Chicora's breast. Joe saw this hasty movement. His eye twinkled as he met

14

Mark's, but he said nothing. He only stared harder at the professor, who was holding the little spray aloft, as he continued talking on rapidly.

"This pretty leetle papilionaceous flower is a very dangerous plant. It is an astragalus. It is the *lathyrus sativus*. In die seventeenth century it work much mischief. Die poebel eat it in dere bread, or in oder ways. It have no bad taste, only sweet an' ver' pleasant. But when it is eat good deal it have ver' bad effects. A great rigidity of die limbs will ensue, causing loss of all die muscular power beyon' die reach of cure. Dere is no premonitory pain; die patient experience only ver' slight diminution of strength, when all of sudden he fine his limbs all rigid an' movement is impossible. You will feed pigeons on die seeds, and dey will walk no more. I have try on die pigeons myself. George, Duke of Wirtemberg, in 1671, publish an edict forbidding die planting of dis pea, an' Leopold, his successor, publish two edicts, in 1705 and 1714, against dis leetle plant, an' now I finds him in America. Is it not *ver' interestin'*?"

The professor was so occupied in pasting down his "interestin'" specimen of "dis leetle pea," that he did not observe Mark's growing pallor, or the expression of intense horror that overspread his sensitive countenance. He shuddered as he looked at the plant which the unconscious professor was quietly spreading out and arranging to suit his fastidious taste.

"My God!" exclaimed horror-stricken Mark.
Cherokee Joe leaned over, and looked at the plant,
neatly stretched out, and stuck in its place by bits
of paper glued with mucilage, lying before the
professor.

"You tink dat so dreadful?" continued the professor. "Dere was plenty of plants in dat leetle
garten worser as dat. Dere was many ver' wicked
plants dere. I haf got dem all. I will show
you."

Mark recovered himself. He dared not say
more. He must take time to think before he acted.
God! it was *awful! awful!* The drops stood upon
his brow.

Joe drew back, after he had taken a careful look
at the plant, with a deep "ugh." Then suddenly
thrusting his red hand before the professor's eyes,
almost knocking off the savant's spectacles, he said,
"What that?"

They were the identical peas he had shown to
Victor in years previous.

The professor took them out of Joe's hand and
examined them.

"Why, dose are the very peas," he said. "That
is the fruit of the *lathyrus sativus.* What are you
to do wid dem? Dey must not be eat."

"Take to Satana," said Joe, as he had said before
to Victor. And Joe gathered the peas up out of
the professor's hand, and replaced them in his skin
pouch.

"Is there *no* antidote for this plant known?" asked Mark at length, when he could command his voice.

"None," replied Römer, laconically. "I have tried every zing on die pigeons. Dey never got any better."

————————

CHAPTER XXVI.

TRAGIC RETRIBUTION.

MARK was greatly troubled at the revelation made so unconsciously to him by Professor Römer. It was impossible to doubt this evidence of the wickedness of the woman who had been his father's wife, and now that the thread of disentanglement had been given into his hands he saw many circumstances in a new aspect to confirm its truth. He remembered the remarks made at the time of his father's death; of Major Flanoy's sudden death; of Chicora's long illness, with its strange, remittent character; his own illness under his stepmother's care; and Mark groaned and shuddered at the fearful atmosphere of crime which surrounded that woman, and in which he, with so many others, had been unconsciously living. Gazing at the spray of pea-blossoms, he wondered at the blindness of himself and of every one else. They might have read about these plants in a hundred books in his grand-father's library—materia medicas, that they had in their hands every day. He got down several; yes, there it was, the description of this *lathyrus sativus*. Why, any child would have known it.

He rang the bell and told Lizbette to send Cherokee Joe to him. Lizbette said "Joe had left at daybreak, and had said he was going to the Nation and would not be back soon again."

Mark was driven back to communings with his own unquiet soul. What was he to do? Expose this woman? or what? She was his father's widow; his father whom she had very probably murdered! She was a female Thug; she was a malignant and poison-breathing creature, who struck in the dark at the very highest and noblest. Yet she was Panola's aunt by the half-blood. Panola! how glad he was that Panola was away from under that pernicious influence which would have not hesitated to attack even her sweet, pure life. *What was he to do?*

Mark asked himself the question every minute. Would it be best to tell his grandfather or not? Should he see the wretched woman privately and tell her how he had discovered her crimes? If he did, and she were to go away, would it not be to carry death and evil wherever she did go? Mark was of a pitiful nature, but he recognized the absolute necessity of human beings destroying all poisonous serpents and serpent-like creatures. Man is obliged to kill them, else they exist only to do evil.

In regard to his own condition Mark had made inquiries, not only from Professor Römer, but in all the books he could find that touched on the subject; there was no known cure for the effects produced by the poisonous pea. He had probably taken very little, not enough to produce the rigidity of the muscles, which was the full effect of the plant. He had probably only received a dose or so as an experiment and test of the power of the plant. Still, it made him more hopeless than ever of his regaining the use of his limbs. Poor Chicora! oh, it was inexpressibly horrible to think of!

Professor Römer departed on the following day, with his trunk filled with specimens, a very happy man, and Mark sat brooding in his chair, most miserable. He had been sitting for hours lost in thought, when he saw a man gallop swiftly up to the door in a very excited manner, who called loudly for Docteur Canonge. His grandfather went out, exchanged a few words with the man, then with a gesture full of horror the old docteur put his hat on his head, mounted the man's horse, and rode away rapidly, leaving the man to follow on foot or as he could. The docteur's horse was grazing in a pasture some little distance off from the house. The man remained talking violently to Lizbette, who listened,

showing by her pantomime that she was greatly
agitated; but at last the man went away, and Lizbette came into Mark with a face full of terror and
excitement.

"Oh! master Mark, there's the dreadfullest thing
has happened! Poor Madame Bolling! she was
well and up at dinner-time, at two o'clock this day,
and now she is lying dead on her bed with her neck
broke, and nobody knows anything about it! She
was walking on the verandah when the servants saw
her last. They were all in the kitchen and the back
part of the house, and at sun-down, when the maid
went to her mistress' room to fix the bed, there was
Madame Bolling lying dead, her head hanging over
the side of the bed, as if somebody had throwed
her on it. There wasn't no sign of scuffling on the
bed or in the room. She was killed on the gallery
and then brought in and flung on the bed. There
was a tiny stream of drops of blood all the way from
the banisters of the gallery to her room. Her head
was flung back as if some one had just forced it
back with his hand until it snapped. There ain't
no sign of a weapon, and no bruises or marks about
her, and there ain't no tracks of a man neither, but
then it is grass lawn all around the verandah, and
that wouldn't show no footprints, nohow. O
Lord! what a country to live in! with wars and
fightings and murders and starvation on all sides
of us!"

This was all Lizbette knew. Mark had to wait until his grandfather returned for further intelligence. The old docteur was very much excited. He confirmed Lizbette's account. This murder had been done in open daylight, and in a house full of servants, and yet no cry for aid had escaped the victim. It was most mysterious. Mrs. Smith and some of the neighbors were there now. Everything had been done, but Madame Bolling was dead.

Mark now told his grandfather about the *lathyrus sativus*, and all he suspected. The old man was overcome with surprise and horror; suspicion flashed across his mind.

"*Where was Cherokee Joe?* No one had seen him for two days past. He was gone to the Nation," everybody said.

Madame Bolling was buried; a marble slab was put over her grave, which nearly covered it, but Mark, driving past there one day, long afterward, saw that the marble slab was nearly concealed from view by the twining, twisting, climbing vines of the poison-pea. *Who* had planted them so thickly upon *that* grave? It was matted with the plant. Mark knew but two persons who were likely to have done this : old Nana for love, Cherokee Joe for hatred.

Joe did not return from the Nation. "He had gone out on the Western prairies," some of his people said ; but an empty purse of deerskin was picked up near the gate of the little churchyard. Lizbette

said that it was " Joe's purse," and she gave it to
Indian Molly, who received it in stolid silence.

" Joe been here lately ? " asked Lizbette.

" Joe gone to Nation," replied Molly, laconically.

" What you think about Madame Bolling's
death ? " asked Lizbette, curiously.

"Ah-skeen-er," laconically replied Molly.

" Where are goin', Molly ? " asked Lizbette.
" I see you've got your pusscoos strapped on your
back, and all those baskets. Those are very pretty
baskets. What will you take for that fanner ? "

Lizbette was always ready to make a bargain.
The " fanner," a large, flat basket, made of very
finely split-cane, woven double, was indeed a beautiful work of Indian art, being extremely fine in the
plaiting, and very tastefully ornamented with colored
borders of red and black dyed splits of the reed.
Molly unstrapped the baskets and sat herself down
on the ground, ready for a trade. Her " pusscoos "
blinked its bright-black eyes when Lizbette chucked
it under the chin.

" That pusscoos is the very image of Joe," said
Lizbette " Wait, I'll give you a flannel gown for
it : bran new red flannel, and a piece of sugar, too.
What will you take for the fanner, Molly ? "

Molly held up her hand with the thumb bent
into the palm.

" Four bits," she said.

" Four bits ! That's too much."

"Fanner vely fine," said Molly; "plenty work to make him."

"But that's too much," argued Lizbette; "I'll give you three bits and a new handkerchief, red and blue—see!"

Molly shook her head, smiling: "No."

"Well, then, three bits and a new tin-cup."

Molly laughed, and repeated her head-shaking of refusal: "No."

"Well, then, three bits and the tin-cup and a bottle of whiskey," said Lizbette.

Molly laughed, with her mouth wider open than ever, showing all her white teeth, but she nodded her head in acquiescence.

"I thought you would," said Lizbette. "Indians does love whiskey—well, I like a little myself sometimes, when I have a misery in my inwards. Molly, wait till I go into the house after the things."

Lizbette turned back from the gate, where this colloquy had taken place, and re-entered the house, whence she soon emerged bearing the bottle of whiskey, the tin-cup, the red flannel and the sugar for the "pusscoos." Molly untied the fanner, and then selecting one of her very prettiest baskets, fitted for holding eggs, she laid it inside the fanner and handed both to Lizbette. "Pusscoos give you this," she said.

Lizbette thanked her heartily, and untying her

own necklace of yellow beads, she added that to the parcel for Molly. Lizbette was very generous, though she liked to trade and beat down prices of things.

"Tankee, Lizbette," said Molly. "Bye, Lizbette, I'm goin' to Nation."

"Good-bye, Molly; good-bye, pusscoos."

"That was a good bargain," remarked Lizbette to herself; "them baskets is worth at least two dollars, specially the fanner. That little pusscoos' eyes are jist like a coon's, they is so bright and so fierce-lookin'!"

"*Ah-skeen-er*, indeed; it's always ah-skeen-er with Injins! and no satisfaction with them. *Ah-skeen-er!* I believe it is '*ah-Joe*' and '*ah-Cherokee*' myself! Injins is so deceitful! That fanner is a real beauty, sure!"

CHAPTER XXVII.

PANOLA IN PARIS.

PANOLA had made a very successful tour through the United States; so much so that her agent considered it advisable that she should go to Europe and try for the laurels that are freely bestowed there upon all real original talent. Panola had

signed the articles of agreement before she learned
of the death of Madame Bolling, though, being the
next of kin, she now inherited all that ill-fated
woman's property. She wrote to Mark, asking him
to take charge of her affairs in Louisiana, as she did
not feel justified in breaking her engagement on an
instant's notice.

The truth was that Panola *was* pleased and interested in the life she was leading. She cared more
for the music of it than the fame; and she looked
forward eagerly to the chance of progress and improvement in her art, which such a tour as that
she had undertaken promised to her. She would
hear all the great musicians of the world, and she
would learn so much. The prospect was very
tempting to her, and fame is pleasant, very pleasant.
She enjoyed being the favorite of the hour. She
was entirely *en rapport* with her public—had a perfect *entente cordiale* towards it en masse—that is,
when it was seated in serried rows on the benches
before her. Then she delighted in the power she
had of bringing smiles or tears to human eyes and
lips. *Individually,* people did not interest Panola.
They fatigued her and occupied the time she preferred to give to her music—that is, unless they
were *real* musicians, and could teach her something;
then Panola would listen to them with eager eyes
and parted lips. She had said once to Victor:
"Music is my life, I think," and it seemed to be

really true. So, in the midst of her brilliant career as an artiste, Panola lived the simplest and quietest life possible. She saw no one, except on business or music. Her faithful maid was always with her, accompanying her to and fro wherever she went.

Of course Panola was often subjected to the attentions which every attractive "diva" receives. She was wondrously beautiful, and beauty attracts as honey does flies and wasps; but it was almost impossible to approach Panola. Gifts she positively rejected even from sovereigns, except a flower, and those she preferred to receive in public. Letters and notes were opened by her secretary, except her private letters from "home." The secretary read them aloud to her as she sat at her breakfast, and jotted down the notes of reply on the outside; so that lovers' billet doux fared badly under these prosaic arrangements. If a billet was extremely original and funny, Panola would sometimes send it to grandpapa Canonge and Mark to read and laugh over.

Panola awoke enthusiasm wherever she went. The wildest and most extravagant tales were circulated about her. She was an "Indian Princess;" she was the heroine of the most romantic histories; there certainly was some mystery about this wonderfully beautiful Louisianaise, who played better on the violin than Gottschalk did on the piano. People took out their atlasses and looked to see in what corner of the earth "Louisiana" was located; and would spread their fingers over that portion of the United States. "Just to think of all this being inhabited by civilized people! It is really wonderful! Such a *new* country, too!" and then they patronized Panola more than ever.

She did not know that they were patronizing her! She thought she was doing them a great favor in playing for them. Her happiest hours were when she stood, violin in hand, before the public. There was no stay in the furore that she inspired, and her agent gathered in gold with both hands. He gave her a fair portion of it, and she sent it all home to "grandpapa and Mark." Her pure, loving heart was anchored there, in that nook of the Louisiana prairie country.

From Paris, where she now was, she wrote thus to Mark:

"I have been here a month—well received. I think the Parisians are kinder to me because I come from a French colony, and they think I am a Creole. They feel a sort of *esprit de famille* in me. The papers are very complimentary; but better than all is the kindly manner in which the great musicians here receive me. They are truly good to me. At my first concert I recognized, in one of the side loges, Victor. It did not agitate me to see him there. I don't believe I should mind meeting him

at all. I only disliked Victor during the brief
period that I was his nominal wife. I suppose you
will think it very strange, but I really believe I
should rather like being on friendly terms with him;
but under the circumstances, that, I suppose, is not
permissible. Natika might not like it. Victor is
looking wretchedly—the ghost of his former self—
and has a bad cough; I often hear it as he attempts
to stifle it. Sometimes he has to go out into the
foyer and cough; then he comes back. You know
he is devoted to music, and he always did like
mine. Poor Victor! he is ill! I wonder where
Natika is? but probably she would not come to
hear me play!

*   *   *   *   *   *   *

"I have heard something of Victor. He is here
alone. Natika is spending the winter in Egypt for
her health, they say. Victor is said to be dying of
consumption—a rapid development of the disease.
Poor fellow!

*   *   *   *   *   *   *

"To-night, in playing, I saw poor Victor rise
and go out to cough; then he came back. He
looked so feeble and so sad. I don't know whether
it was right or wrong in me, but my heart ached for
the poor suffering fellow. His eyes are more like
yours than ever, Mark; they look larger and deeper
in expression than they used to do.

"I was called back three times after every piece,

and at the last encore I signed to have my violin
handed back to me. It was brought. When I took
it again in my hands, smiling, the house rose. You
never heard such a noise as they did make; but at
the first scrape of the bow all was still. I played,
for the first time in Europe, an improvisation. I
played it for Victor I played some things he used
to sing for us—some things mamma liked—as
tenderly as I could; then I played some modula-
tions, and got into 'Dixie' and the 'Bonnie Blue
Flag;' and wound up with an allegro on the corn
song of the negroes, and the extravaganza of the
'Arkansas Traveller.' Victor knew then that I had
recognized him. He waved his hand sadly, and
put it up over his eyes—I think he wept. I quitted
the stage, and the curtain dropped. As I was leaving
the dressing-room to return to my lodgings, accompanied, as usual, by my good Ellen, a note was
handed me from Victor—here it is; I send it to you
to read:

"'PANOLA:—I think, from your music to-night,
that you have forgiven me. You can recall the past
without pain or anger. I know that means
that you never did love me much. If you
loved me you would not have forgiven or forgotten
so readily. So that emboldens me—as mortifying
as the facts may be to any man's vanity—yet it emboldens me to approach you. They tell me I am

dying. I suppose I am. I suffer enough, God knows! and I feel so utterly forlorn and so lonely. I can't tell you what I felt in hearing the sound again of your Straduarius, and of the intense longing for home and childhood's friends that came over me when I saw you. I have heard nothing from Louisiana for so long—grandpapa and Mark have thrown us off, you know—Natika and me. Some old Roman, I don't remember who—Coriolanus, I think —said, "It is only in old age that one feels how bitter it is to be an exile from one's country." Oh, Panola! illness and pain act like old age for me! I can't tell you how I long and yearn for home, and for the old familiar faces. It would be a charity in you to receive me for an hour. May I come? If so, send a note to Numero 11, Rue St. Honore.   "'VICTOR.'

"I wrote him to come the next morning at eleven o'clock.

*   *   *   *   *   *   *

"Punctually at eleven o'clock Victor entered my little salon. Ellen was sewing in the adjoining apartment, with the door opened between us. Victor was very much agitated—more than I was. He kissed my hand in silence as I extended it to him; then he began to cough. I pushed an easy-chair towards him, and stirred up the fire to make it blaze. Victor threw himself in the chair.

15

"'You see me a poor wreck, Panola,' he said. His face is very gaunt and emaciated. His eyes are like deep caverns in his face.

"I said, 'Does your cough hurt you much, Victor?'

"'At times,' he replied. Then we both sat silent for a while. I did not feel embarrassed, but I felt so sorry, and very earnest. There was no place for coquetry or trifling between us two.

"Victor did not speak; he sat looking into the fire. I let him alone. I took up some embroidery I was doing—a sofa-cushion for *you*, Mark—and there we sat as composedly as we used to do: he lying back in the chair, and I sewing. I got up and pushed a stool under his feet. 'It will be more comfortable,' I said.

"'Thanks. What are you making, Panola?'

"'A sofa-cushion for Mark.'

"'It is very pretty.' Then he glanced around the room and spied the large photographs of you and grandpapa that I carry about, and call my Lares.

"'Those are good likenesses,' he said. 'When did you hear last from home?'

"I told him. Then I got out the last package of letters and read him all that I thought would interest him from them.

"He asked me to let him see the last from grandpapa. I gave it to him. He read it over again, and kissed it, as he folded it up to return to me.

" 'The dear, good old man !' he cried. Then we started in a stream of talk. He had so many questions to ask, and I so much to tell. He was surprised to hear of poor aunt Bolling's strange death. I wonder what mysterious enemy she could have had? You never gave me a clear account of it all, somehow.

" Victor cheered up wonderfully, and at times would show glimpses of his old self, in light mocking speeches. Indeed, I found myself laughing and scolding at him, just as we used to do before all that terrible folly came between us. He stretched himself out with his feet to the fire, and seemed really comfortable. I made him a nice milk punch, with real country cream in it, and gave him some lunch before he left. He ate with appetite—he said more than he had had for a long time. I had a musical engagement after that. So I told him he must go; I had work to do. He got up instantly.

" 'I may come again, Panola?'

" 'You may come when you like, Victor, in reasonable hours,' I said. 'I am often busy. When I can see you, I will; but of course I must do my work. But you will understand that.'

" 'Of course,' he replied; 'it is very good of you to let me come at all.'

" He has been coming nearly every day. I see him whenever I can, and try to do all I can for him. I have told him to write to you and to grandpapa. Answer him kindly, dear Mark—dearest grandpapa: the poor fellow is so ill.

"Natika is in Egypt, with her relatives. Victor does not speak of her much to me, of course; though he might do so if he liked; it wouldn't hurt me at all."

Victor wrote:

"PARIS, 18—.

"DEAR MARK:—Panola encourages me to write to you, and to dear grandpapa. She has doubtless told you the condition of health in which she has found me. She is so compassionate and good. There is no use in referring to the past; that is dead and gone. Your prophecy was true, Mark, and has been so painfully fulfilled! I am dying with consumption; but that is not the worst of it, Mark: I am dying *alone*, except for the attendance of hirelings—services that money will always command, you know. It is a sorrowful fact which forced itself upon my most unwilling mind: but I am become a source of horror and disgust to my poor wife. I suppose she can't help natural idiosyncrasy, but Natika hates sickness, and calamity, and physical disease. She can't help it. Even when she would try to conceal it and to repress the shrinking from me after my health commenced to fail, I saw it plainly—she shuddered at my touch. She turned pale when she would inhale my breath. It seemed poisonous and noxious to her. There was an innate repulsion towards illness and sick people. I feel sorry for her. All the horrid paraphernalia of confirmed chronic invalidism, the fevers and the coughing, and the weakness—all are hateful to her. She could not hide her repugnance from me. I tried to incommode her as little as possible; but, finding her so intensely bored, I persuaded her to go to Egypt for the winter. She is not very strong, and the air of the desert is said to be good for delicate lungs. She was very glad to go. It is an immense relief to her. I promised to go to the south of France, or to Madeira. But I have not gone. I have such a longing for *home*. I wish I might come. Panola thinks you would let me.

"Of course you know what a world-famous diva Panola is. The people go mad over her. She deserves it. She is, if anything, more beautiful than ever, and she improves every day in her playing; she studies so hard.

"Oh, Mark! what a fool I was! But I dare not speak of the past, 'when, like the base Judæan, I threw away a pearl richer than all my tribe.' By the way, does that mean Judas Iscariot, or Herod the king, when he killed Mariamne?

"Talking of killing reminds me of Madame Bolling. I have no doubt there was retributive justice in her end, though Panola don't seem to understand about it exactly. I must tell you that 'zose Injuns'—as grandpapa calls them—the Cherokees, Panola's respectable relatives, have not forgotten me. Every year I have received through the post a peculiar letter, which, when opened, contains nothing but a very correctly drawn rattlesnake coiled to spring Whoever drew it has caught the reptilish characteristics admirably.

"I have quite a little package of these epistles, which I have carefully filed away, but which certainly will not deter me from returning to America. Indeed, as matters are now, I believe I had rather make a finis at once, through the instrumentality of an Indian arrow or tomahawk, than to shake myself to pieces, gradually, with coughing. Day and night, I have no rest. I wonder if grandpapa could prescribe something to alleviate my wretchedness. Panola cooks me up messes that seem to help me a little, temporarily. Do write soon to me. I am famished for news from you and grandpapa. Your loving and miserable

"VICTOR."

Victor to Mark, later.

"PARIS, 18—.

"DEAREST MARK:—Your kind letter, containing the few precious words from grandpapa, reached me only a few minutes ago. Thanks, a thousand thanks, that you will receive back your prodigal, alas! not like the younger son Odin, in grandpapa's story—bringing precious gifts in his hands—but sick and worn and weary : coming home only to die.

"Dear Mark, I am growing weaker day by day. Panola, who has been as good to me as an angel, says she will cancel her engagements here to accompany me home. She insists upon it, and I—dear Mark, don't despise me too much—I am so weak I cannot but accept this sacrifice from the woman I have wronged so much. I know I have no right to do it, but Panola is a part of home—that home I yearn for so much—and it is such a consolation to have her near me. I suffer a good deal, and she seems to know how to help me, in a thousand little ways of womanly ministration.

"I never told you, Mark, about my greatest sorrow here in the birth and death of my little child. It was a terrible grief and disappointment to me at the time, but I think of it now with calmness, seeing I shall so soon be with my little daughter in the better life.

"Natika never liked children, and she was not pleased when our little girl came. She was very ill at the time of its birth. She had over-exerted herself at a fête at Compeigne, where she had been invited by the empress, and where she insisted upon going, in spite of my earnest entreaties not to. She danced a great deal, until she was overcome by fatigue and heat, and she fainted on her way home from the imperial ball. Her dress was made too tight and too elaborate, in order to conceal her form. The consequence was, the premature birth of my child. It lived three days. It was very beautiful; and my whole soul went out towards it. My poor little daughter! It was baptized Victorine. Its mother never noticed it much. I carried it to her bedside when it was a day old, to show it to her, but she merely glanced at it and said it was 'a nice little thing,' and hoped the nurse was a good one.

"I assured her it was the best nurse I could procure in all Paris.

"She smiled languidly, 'That's good.'

"I said timidly to her, 'Wouldn't you like to have the babe lie by you a while, dear?'

"She said, 'No; she was not used to babies. She might hurt it.'

"I took my child away. Natika never loved me, Mark. I know that now. She did not love our child either. Oh, my God! I am fearfully punished!

"My little child became ill, and after watching by it for two days and nights, I saw it lie dead before me. I suppose it inherited no strength to live from us two miserable parents.

"I told Natika our babe was dead. I thought she might like to look at it once more before the grave closed over its sweet face. But she said, 'No, it made her shudder to think of anything born of her being dead. It seemed as if part of herself was being buried.' She turned so pale and seemed to suffer so much that I vowed mentally never to speak of the child again to her; and I never have. I have ordered Victorine's remains to be sent home to you, dearest Mark. I had it deposited in a vault in Père la Chaise, with that intention. You will bury my child among her ancestors for my sake. I shall leave here next week; pray God for me that I may live to see your face once more, and dear grandpapa's.   "YOUR VICTOR."

CHAPTER XXVIII.

VICTOR'S DEATH.

"NEW YORK, 18—.

"DEAR MARK:—You see by the date that I have arrived here. We had a tedious and tempestuous voyage, which increased poor Victor's sufferings; but he bore it all so patiently. He had such a sweet temper naturally, and so gay and bright, and really an affectionate, true heart. Poor Victor! He was so anxious to live to reach 'home,' and grandpapa and you. But, oh, Mark! it seemed cruel that he should die just the day before we got to New York! It was so hard! I weep to think of it. However it has to be borne. I am so glad that I persisted in coming with him. I don't know what he would have done without my good Ellen and me. He was so weak. But he would laugh and say funny things to the very last. The day before he died he was sitting up on the deck in a sheltered place. I was sitting by him. Ellen was below preparing some little dainty for him, when a lady came up and said, kindly:

"'How is your brother to-day, madame?'

"Victor answered himself, 'that he was more comfortable.' Then, when she had walked away, he said:

"'What relation am I to you, Panola?'

"I really was nonplussed for the instant, but, recovering myself, I said:

"'In our Indian tongue I should call you "my brother."'

"'Should you?' he said. 'And yet, how different it might have all been, Panola.'

"'It is better as it is,' I replied. 'I have always known that.'

"'Yes, you love your Straduarius better than you do me, and Mark better than the Straduarius, and grandpapa better than Mark.'

"I smiled. Then Victor said, very seriously:

"'Panola, do you know that I could have been madly in love with one other woman in the world besides my infatuation for Natika; nay, even in spite of it, had the fates been propitious?'

"'I know, Victor,' I said; 'it was with mamma.'

"'Yes. I *could* have loved her. I expect she died cursing *me* too, did not she?'

"I could not reply. I expect my mother did.

"'Well, it does not matter much now. In a very little while all will be clear between your mother and myself. I shall have an explanation with her pretty soon, in the "land of the hereafter," as you Indians call it.'

"Victor used to think more seriously than he talked of things, Mark. He used to think a great deal, and I believe he often prayed; but it was his way to talk lightly and gayly about serious matters. Victor had some lovely traits of character.

"He died quite calmly, whilst sleeping. I will give you all the details when we meet, so that you can write them to Natika. I found a thick letter, sealed and addressed to her, in Victor's writing-desk. I forwarded it as soon as we arrived, with a newspaper containing the notice of his death at sea.

"The remains have gone on to Louisiana. I find myself so much fatigued and exhausted by watching, anxiety and grief, that I must stay here a while to rest, before I renew my travels. My engagement is ended, and I long for home; so you may expect me soon. Grandpapa will have to take me in until I can provide myself with an establishment in my own long-deserted huge house. His and your

"PANOLA."

The group of friends stood around Victor's open grave. The words " Earth to earth, and dust to dust" had just been uttered, and the earth was being cast gently upon the coffin, when a woman made her way through the small group to the side of the grave. She had a blanket pinned over her head. She put this aside, and revealed the dusky features of Indian Molly, Cherokee Joe's wife. She knelt, and laid upon the descending coffin a hatchet whose handle was streaked and painted with red, and a pipe tufted with red feathers; then she rose up and glided swiftly away. Death had forestalled the vengeance of the Cherokee. The grave was filled in silence, and the vengeful weapons were buried with Victor.

CHAPTER XXIX.

LOVE'S MIRACLE.

IT was the very brightest and most sunshiny of days, and the mocking-birds were trying to kill themselves with singing, when Panola drove up to the door of Docteur Canonge's house. The old man was at the gate, to clasp "his darling" in his arms; and Lizbette too, who not only hugged Panola but also Ellen in the fervor of her welcome. Ellen did not half like being kissed by the old mulattress, but Panola returned her embrace very warmly; then leaving them all far behind her—for hers were the footsteps of youth and joy—Panola sprang up the steps and into Mark's study. There he sat in the old place. Without a thought of wrong, Panola rushed towards him with her outstretched arms.

"Mark! dear Mark!"

" Panola!"

With that word, Mark, for the first time in his life, clasped to his heart the one woman he loved. He strained her to his bosom with an immense passion he could not control for an instant. Panola recoiled, and seemed to struggle to free herself from that passionate clasp. The meaning burst upon her. It was only for an instant. The next, her arms were about his neck, and her lips turned up to meet his kiss—one supreme moment of bliss after long parting. Panola heard grandpapa coming, but she did not move; she lay still in Mark's embrace.

Joy, intense and beyond expression, thrilled through Mark. Life seemed to pour in an immense wave of emotion and vital force through every nerve, every muscle. His heart beat like a drum; its pulsations could be heard.

Docteur Canonge stopped short at the door, transfixed by the sudden revelation betrayed by the grouping of the actors in this little domestic drama.

"Ah! vat is dis?" he exclaimed.

Mark laughed aloud. He was radiant in his happiness. He gently lifted Panola from his bosom.

"She will never leave us again, grandpapa," said Mark.

"No, never!" replied Panola, energetically throwing herself upon the old man's breast. She wept a few tears of joy.

"Grandpapa! Panola!" cried Mark, suddenly, lifting himself up from his chair, by resting his hands on its arms; "Grandpapa, give me your hands. It seems to me as if a new vigor was pouring through my nerves! I think—I believe—Panola! Let me try—help me to try to *walk.*"

The two sprang towards him. They seized his hands. They drew him to his feet. Mark stood tottering with their arms around him. Panola kissed his hands violently. "Try, Mark! dear Mark, try! One step, Mark!" Poising one hand upon her shoulder, and resting the other upon his grandfather's arm, Mark, by an immense effort, lifted his foot and made one step forward, then another. They sustained him, their very souls hanging upon his movements.

"Grasp my hand firmly, Panola!" he cried. "Life power seems to flow into me from the clasp of your hands!"

They held him firmly. He walked across the room to the window, then back.

"Now," he said, "let go my hands." They dropped his hands. Docteur Canonge was weeping. Panola walked away to the other side of the room, stopped, stood leaning forward with her arms extended wide, as a mother does when her child makes its first tottering steps. There was a whole heaven of love and strength in her eyes. "Mark, my love! Mark!" she said, softly.

Mark laughed in his wild, joyful excitement. Throwing his head back, he stood erect and walked firmly though carefully across the room, and caught Panola again in his arms; covering her face with kisses, he bowed his head above hers, hidden upon his breast.

"My God! I thank thee!" he said.

Docteur Canonge stole out of the room; but a half hour later, he poked his head inside of the doorway, his eyes very red from weeping for joy, and he called out in quavering tones:

"Mark, I muss apologize to zie manes of my good brudder Jacob! A wise man was Jacob! He know how to make you get well again. He was better docteur as me! I have been most ungrateful to Jacob. You will have all zie money, and zie Charitee will go beg. How wise was Jacob!"

CHAPTER XXX.

THE CHEROKEE CHIEF.

MARK and Panola walked to the little church, when they were married, shortly after her return. Panola had no trousseau, but she had plenty of very nice clothes she had brought with her from Paris. She had not even a proper wedding-gown, but she wore a very pretty pink silk one, and her wreath was made of *real* roses and unmedicated orange flowers.

Satana came from the Nation to give the bride away, and Mark's curiosity in regard to this famous chief was fully gratified. Satana was dressed like a Christian, in the finest linen and broadcloth. He wore lemon-colored gloves, and a high silk hat, which he held gracefully in his hand, and he behaved altogether very much like the Christians who surrounded him on this memorable occasion. He was a very handsome, tall half-breed, and had graduated at Yale College. So, as Lizbette said, *"he knew very well what was what."* He presented Panola with some handsome jewels, and the prettiest fan that Tyndale, of New York, could manufacture. And Panola found upon her dressing-table her *lost* golden rattlesnake.

After the wedding, when he was smoking a cigar

on the verandah with Mark and Docteur Canonge, and they spoke of "the peas" and "the powder" that Cherokee Joe had given to Satana, his chief, Satana said that Cherokee Joe had seen Madame Bolling mix the powders in some lemonades that were prepared for Major Flanoy. That he had observed the expression of her face, which he did not like. So he watched her and he distrusted her. He stole one of the powders out of her dressing-room at the Pavilion.

Shortly after Chicora was taken ill, in prowling about, watching madame, he had seen Nana pounding the peas in a mortar. He managed to secure a few of them also. Then he tried to get some information about the two articles. He did not succeed in this, before the visit of Professor Römer; further than this, and that Joe had brought the powder and the peas to *him*, Satana would not say if he knew. No one could guess anything from his imperturbable countenance. He quietly parried any further questioning. He said Joe was gone far out west on the hunting-grounds of the tribe.

Mark could scarcely persuade himself to believe that this quiet, elegant *gentleman*, who sat smoking his cigar so gracefully, was the terrible chief who had led his tribe during the Confederate war, in all the glory of red paint and war feathers, by the side of Colonel Albert Pike. He was as gentle now "as a sucking-dove." But the other Indians, enemies of

16

his tribe, knew Satana very well. He grew weary occasionally of the tedium of peace and civilization, and when he did put on his leggings and war-crown, the Comanches and Apaches sent their runners to summon all their bravest allies. It required no telegraph to announce that *Satana was on the war-path.* The "smoke beacons" of the Indians leaped instantly from every hill top.

Satana's warriors were no longer armed with the traditional bow and arrow, or the tomahawk. They had very excellent Henry and Spencer breech-loading rifles, and the latest improved patents of revolvers. Satana was telling Mark now about a very fine "Greener shot-gun of laminated steel" he had had made in England, at a cost of four hundred and fifty dollars. He said he liked it better than "one he had got from Lieges." Pinned carefully in the buttonhole of his black broadcloth satin-lined coat Satana wore a pretty spray of bright pea blossoms. He had gathered them as the wedding party passed out of the churchyard. Docteur Canonge saw him stoop down, for an instant, as the cortege passed by Madame Bolling's grave, and pluck a flaunting branch of the luxuriant vines.

He carelessly asked Docteur Canonge for its true botanical name. That night, after he had retired to his apartment, Satana put the faded flowers into an envelope, sealed it, and wrote in pencil upon the envelope these words:

THE LATHYRUS SATIVUS,

OR

CHICKEN VETCHLING:

FROM THE GRAVE OF MADAME BOLLING,

added the date, and put the envelope into his handsome travelling-bag. The veneering of civilization had made the Cherokees a more agreeable people to their white neighbors; but there were malicious persons who said that in the privacy of the Cherokee houses there were Bluebeard cupboards, where all trophies were carefully preserved; and that there were still some nicely dried scalps of white men, even in Satana's mahogany wardrobes, as trophies from the recent war.

The Cherokees often assured their pale-faced brothers, "that although their skins were red, their hearts were all white." But Docteur Canonge used to shrug his shoulders at that. He said, "Where the blood remained *unmixed*, that their hearts were as red as their faces." But then Docteur Canonge was a very obstinate physiologist, and Docteur Canonge also said, in speaking of the mustang or Indian pony, "that *it* had improved upon its ancestor, the Andalusian barb, both in bottom, swiftness, and docility." Altogether Docteur Canonge considered "a well-mounted Indian warrior, like Satana, a formidable and unpleasant antagonist."

Mark and Panola made a large votive offering to

the *Charity*, when Mark took possession of uncle Jacob's estate.

Panola gave a beautiful memorial window to the church, where Victor and his little child and her parents were buried.

"Mark," said Panola, "there is nothing so sad to me as the failure of such a life as Victor's. He never had justice done him by any of us. I did not love him as much as I ought. Natika, to whom he gave his truest devotion, did not love him. All the women and all the men he knew disappointed him, except grandpapa. The only human being who really comprehended Victor and fully appreciated him was mamma, and you know how that was. She would not have died so angry at him if she had not loved him. I was not at all angry. I was glad when he went away. Ah, there is nothing of any value without love. I have had fame and plenty of money, but *love* is the only thing of any worth—*love*, whether it be in the forest or in the palace."

Mark stopped her mouth with a kiss. He approved of her logic, as well as of her practice. Grandpapa Canonge still gives soirées, and he and Madame Duplessis mère always lead the "cotillon," and will continue to do so till they are a century old.

The sunshine falls brilliantly over the churchyard. The marble tombs of Victor and Chicora are glitteringly white in the splendor of its light. On the topmost bough of the oak tree, whose waving shadows chequer the graves, a mocking bird is singing, "Sweetie, sweetie, Bob White, Bob White," and it ends its cadence with the three notes of the troopiall. It had learned its singing lesson during the eventful years. In the depths of the oak bough, its mate sits on a nest of young birds, and replies to the bursts of music with a short cry of *"Chic! chic! chicora! chic! chic! chicora! chic! chic!"* And the young ones respond, " chee-chee-squah," as they stretch wide their yawning bills for the striped caterpillars their parents gather up to feed them with. The early peas and the strawberries are devoured more freely than ever out of Docteur Canonge's garden. The birds are still predatory as Indians in their habits.

THE END.

T. B. PETERSON AND BROTHERS' PUBLICATIONS.

MRS. EMMA D. E. N. SOUTHWORTH'S WORKS.

Complete in forty-two large duodecimo volumes, bound in morocco cloth, gilt back, price $1.75 each; or $73.50 a set, each set is put up in a neat box.

Self-Raised; From the Depths..	$1 75	The Fatal Marriage,	$1 75
Ishmael; or, In the Depths,	1 75	The Deserted Wife,	1 75
The Fatal Secret,	1 75	The Fortune Seeker,	1 75
How He Won Her,	1 75	The Bridal Eve,	1 75
Fair Play,	1 75	The Lost Heiress,	1 75
The Spectre Lover,	1 75	The Two Sisters,	1 75
Victor's Triumph,	1 75	Lady of the Isle,	1 75
A Beautiful Fiend,	1 75	Prince of Darkness,	1 75
The Artist's Love,	1 75	The Three Beauties,	1 75
A Noble Lord,	1 75	Vivia; or the Secret of Power,	1 75
Lost Heir of Linlithgow,	1 75	Love's Labor Won,	1 75
Tried for her Life,	1 75	The Gipsy's Prophecy,	1 75
Cruel as the Grave,	1 75	Retribution,	1 75
The Maiden Widow,	1 75	Haunted Homestead,	1 75
The Family Doom,	1 75	Wife's Victory,	1 75
The Bride's Fate,	1 75	Allworth Abbey,	1 75
The Changed Brides,	1 75	The Mother-in-Law,	1 75
Fallen Pride,	1 75	India; Pearl of Pearl River,	1 75
The Christmas Guest,	1 75	Curse of Clifton,	1 75
The Widow's Son,	1 75	Discarded Daughter	1 75
The Bride of Llewellyn,	1 75	The Mystery of Dark Hollow,	1 75
The Missing Bride; or, Miriam, the Avenger,			1 75

Above are each in cloth, or each one is in paper cover, at $1.50 each.

MRS. ANN S. STEPHENS' WORKS.

Complete in twenty-three large duodecimo volumes, bound in morocco cloth, gilt back, price $1.75 each; or $41.25 a set, each set is put up in a neat box.

Norston's Rest,	$1 75	The Soldiers' Orphans,	$1 75
Bertha's Engagement,	1 75	A Noble Woman,	1 75
Bellehood and Bondage,	1 75	Silent Struggles	1 75
The Old Countess,	1 75	The Rejected Wife,	1 75
Lord Hope's Choice,	1 75	The Wife's Secret,	1 75
The Reigning Belle,	1 75	Mary Derwent,	1 75
Palaces and Prisons,	1 75	Fashion and Famine,	1 75
Married in Haste,	1 75	The Curse of Gold,	1 75
Wives and Widows,	1 75	Mabel's Mistake,	1 75
Ruby Gray's Strategy	1 75	The Old Homestead,	1 75
Doubly False,.... 1 75	The Heiress,.... 1 75	The Gold Brick,... 1 75	

Above are each in cloth, or each one is in paper cover, at $1.50 each.

MRS. C. A. WARFIELD'S WORKS.

Complete in nine large duodecimo volumes, bound in morocco cloth, gilt back, price $1.75 each; or $15.75 a set, each set is put up in a neat box.

The Cardinal's Daughter,	$1 75	Miriam's Memoirs,	$1 75
Ferne Fleming,	1 75	Monfort Hall,	1 75
The Household of Bouverie,	1 75	Sea and Shore,	1 75
A Double Wedding	1 75	Hester Howard's Temptation,	1 75
Lady Ernestine; or, The Absent Lord of Rocheforte,			1 75

MRS. CAROLINE LEE HENTZ'S WORKS.

Green and Gold Edition. Complete in twelve volumes, in green morocco cloth, price $1.75 each; or $21.00 a set, each set is put up in a neat box.

Ernest Linwood,..................$1 75	Love after Marriage..............$1 75
The Planter's Northern Bride,.. 1 75	Eoline; or Magnolia Vale,..... 1 75
Courtship and Marriage......... 1 75	The Lost Daughter.............. 1 75
Rena; or, the Snow Bird,...... 1 75	The Banished Son,.............. 1 75
Marcus Warland.................. 1 75	Helen and Arthur.............. 1 75
Linda; or, the Young Pilot of the Belle Creole............................ 1 75
Robert Graham; the Sequel to "Linda; or Pilot of Belle Creole.".... 1 75

Above are each in cloth, or each one is in paper cover, at $1.50 each.

BEST COOK BOOKS PUBLISHED.

Every housekeeper should possess at least one of the following Cook Books, as they would save the price of it in a week's cooking.

The Queen of the Kitchen. Containing 1007 Old Maryland
Family Receipts for Cooking..Cloth, $1 75
Miss Leslie's New Cookery Book,..................................Cloth, 1 75
Mrs. Hale's New Cook Book,...Cloth, 1 75
Petersons' New Cook Book...Cloth, 1 75
Widdifield's New Cook Book,..Cloth, 1 75
Mrs. Goodfellow's Cookery as it Should Be,....................Cloth, 1 75
The National Cook Book. By a Practical Housewife,.........Cloth, 1 75
The Young Wife's Cook Book.......................................Cloth, 1 75
Miss Leslie's New Receipts for Cooking,........................Cloth, 1 75
Mrs. Hale's Receipts for the Million,.............................Cloth, 1 75
The Family Save-All. By author of "National Cook Book," Cloth, 1 75
Francatelli's Modern Cook. With the most approved methods of
French, English, German, and Italian Cookery. With Sixty-two
Illustrations. One volume of 600 pages, bound in morocco cloth, 5 00

JAMES A. MAITLAND'S WORKS.

Complete in seven large duodecimo volumes, bound in cloth, gilt back, price $1.75 each; or $12.25 a set, each set is put up in a neat box.

The Watchman,..................$1 75	Diary of an Old Doctor,........$1 75
The Wanderer,................... 1 75	Sartaroe,........................... 1 75
The Lawyer's Story............. 1 75	The Three Cousins.............. 1 75
The Old Patroon; or the Great Van Broek Property,................... 1 75

Above are each in cloth, or each one is in paper cover, at $1.50 each.

T. ADOLPHUS TROLLOPE'S WORKS.

Complete in seven large duodecimo volumes, bound in cloth, gilt back, price $1.75 each; or $12.25 a set, each set is put up in a neat box.

The Sealed Packet,................$1 75	Dream Numbers,..................$1 75
Garstang Grange,................ 1 75	Beppo, the Conscript,............ 1 75
Leonora Casaloni,... 1 75	Gemma.......... 1 75	Marietta............ 1 75

Above are each in cloth, or each one is in paper cover, at $1.50 each.

FREDRIKA BREMER'S WORKS.

Complete in six large duodecimo volumes, bound in cloth, gilt back, price $1.75 each; or $10.50 a set, each set is put up in a neat box.

Father and Daughter,...........$1 75	The Neighbors,..................$1 75
The Four Sisters................ 1 75	The Home,...................... 1 75

Above are each in cloth, or each one is in paper cover, at $1.50 each.

Life in the Old World. In two volumes, cloth, price, ... 3 50

☞ Above Books will be sent, postage paid, on receipt of Retail Price,
by T. B. Peterson & Brothers, Philadelphia, Pa.

MISS ELIZA A. DUPUY'S WORKS.

Complete in fourteen large duodecimo volumes, bound in morocco cloth, gilt back, price $1.75 each; or $24.50 a set, each set is put up in a neat box.

A New Way to Win a Fortune	$1 75	Why Did He Marry Her?	$1 75
The Discarded Wife,	1 75	Who Shall be Victor?	1 75
The Clandestine Marriage,	1 75	The Mysterious Guest,	1 75
The Hidden Sin,	1 75	Was He Guilty?	1 75
The Dethroned Heiress,	1 75	The Cancelled Will,	1 75
The Gipsy's Warning,	1 75	The Planter's Daughter,	1 75
All For Love,	1 75	Michael Rudolph,	1 75

Above are each in cloth, or each one is in paper cover, at $1.50 each.

EMERSON BENNETT'S WORKS.

Complete in seven large duodecimo volumes, bound in cloth, gilt back, price $1.75 each; or $12.25 a set, each set is put up in a neat box.

The Border Rover,	$1 75	Bride of the Wilderness,	$1 75
Clara Moreland,	1 75	Ellen Norbury,	1 75
The Orphan's Trials,	1 75	Kate Clarendon,	1 75
Viola; or Adventures in the Far South-West,			1 75

Above are each in cloth, or each one is in paper cover, at $1.50 each.

The Heiress of Bellefonte, ... 75 | The Pioneer's Daughter, ... 75

DOESTICKS' WORKS.

Complete in four large duodecimo volumes, bound in cloth, gilt back, price $1.75 each; or $7.00 a set, each set is put up in a neat box.

Doesticks' Letters,	$1 75	The Elephant Club,	$1 75
Plu-Ri-Bus-Tah,	1 75	Witches of New York,	1 75

Above are each in cloth, or each one is in paper cover, at $1.50 each.

GREEN'S WORKS ON GAMBLING.

Complete in four large duodecimo volumes, bound in cloth, gilt back, price $1.75 each; or $7.00 a set, each set is put up in a neat box.

Gambling Exposed,	$1 75	Reformed Gambler,	$1 75
The Gambler's Life,	1 75	Secret Band of Brothers,	1 75

Above are each in cloth, or each one is in paper cover, at $1.50 each.

DOW'S PATENT SERMONS.

Complete in four large duodecimo volumes, bound in cloth, gilt back, price $1.50 each; or $6.00 a set, each set is put up in a neat box.

Dow's Patent Sermons, 1st Series, cloth,	$1 50	Dow's Patent Sermons, 3d Series, cloth,	$1 50
Dow's Patent Sermons, 2d Series, cloth,	1 50	Dow's Patent Sermons, 4th Series, cloth,	1 50

Above are each in cloth, or each one is in paper cover, at $1.00 each.

WILKIE COLLINS' BEST WORKS.

Basil; or, The Crossed Path..$1 50 | The Dead Secret. 12mo........$1 50

Above are each in one large duodecimo volume, bound in cloth.

The Dead Secret, 8vo	50	The Queen's Revenge,	75
Basil; or, the Crossed Path,	75	Miss or Mrs?	50
Hide and Seek,	75	Mad Monkton,	50
After Dark,	75	Sights a-Foot,	50
The Stolen Mask,	25	The Yellow Mask.... 25	Sister Rose,... 25

The above books are each issued in paper cover, in octavo form.

FRANK FORRESTER'S SPORTING BOOK.

Frank Forrester's Sporting Scenes and Characters. By Henry William Herbert. With Illustrations by Darley. Two vols., cloth,...$4 00

☞ **Above Books will be sent, postage paid, on receipt of Retail Price, by T. B. Peterson & Brothers, Philadelphia, Pa.**

WORKS BY THE VERY BEST AUTHORS.

The following books are each issued in one large duodecimo volume, bound in cloth, at $1.75 each, or each one is in paper cover, at $1.50 each.

The Initials. A Love Story. By Baroness Tautphœus............$1 75
Married Beneath Him. By author of "Lost Sir Massingberd,"...... 1 75
Lost Sir Massingberd. By author of "Married Beneath Him,"......... 1 75
The Clyffards of Clyffe. by author of "Lost Sir Massingberd,"...... 1 75
Margaret Maitland. By Mrs. Oliphant, author of "Zaidee,"......... 1 75
Family Pride. By author of "Pique," "Family Secrets," etc......... 1 75
Self-Sacrifice. By author of "Margaret Maitland." etc............... 1 75
The Woman in Black. A Companion to the "Woman in White,"... 1 75
A Woman's Thoughts about Women. By Miss Muloch,............... 1 75
Flirtations in Fashionable Life. By Catharine Sinclair,............... 1 75
False Pride; or, Two Ways to Matrimony. A Charming Book,...... 1 75
Rose Douglas. A Companion to "Family Pride," and "Self Sacrifice," 1 75
Family Secrets. A Companion to "Family Pride," and "Pique,"... 1 75
The Heiress in the Family. By Mrs. Mackenzie Daniel,............... 1 75
Popery Exposed. An Exposition of Popery as it was and is, ... 1 75
The Heiress of Sweetwater. A Charming Novel,..................... 1 75
Woman's Wrong. By Mrs. Eiloart, author of "St. Bede's,"............ 1 75
The Autobiography of Edward Wortley Montagu, ... 1 75
A Lonely Life. By the author of "Wise as a Serpent," etc............. 1 75
The Macdermots of Ballycloran. By Anthony Trollope,............... 1 75
The Forsaken Daughter. A Companion to "Linda," 1 75
Love and Liberty. A Revolutionary Story. By Alexander Dumas, 1 75
The Morrisons. By Mrs. Margaret Hosmer,..................... 1 75
My Son's Wife. By author of "Caste," "Mr. Arle," etc............... 1 75
The Rich Husband. By author of "George Geith," 1 75
Harem Life in Egypt and Constantinople. By Emmeline Lott,...... 1 75
The Rector's Wife; or, the Valley of a Hundred Fires,............... 1 75
Woodburn Grange. A Novel. By William Howitt, ... 1 75
Country Quarters. By the Countess of Blessington,............... 1 75
Out of the Depths. The Story of a "Woman's Life,"............... 1 75
The Devoted Bride. A Story of the Heart. By St. George Tucker, 1 75
The Coquette: or, the Life and Letters of Eliza Wharton,............ 1 75
The Pride of Life. A Story of the Heart. By Lady Jane Scott,..... 1 75
The Lost Beauty. By a Noted Lady of the Spanish Court,............ 1 75
My Hero. By Mrs. Forrester. A Charming Love Story,............ 1 75
The Quaker Soldier. A Revolutionary Romance. By Judge Jones,..... 1 75
The Man of the World. An Autobiography. By William North,... 1 75
The Queen's Favorite; or, The Price of a Crown. A Love Story,... 1 75
Self Love; or, The Afternoon of Single and Married Life, ... 1 75
Memoirs of Vidocq, the French Detective. His Life and Adventures, 1 75
Cumors. "The Man of the Second Empire." By Octave Feuillet,.. 1 75
The Belle of Washington. With her Portrait. By Mrs. N. P. Lasselle, 1 75
Cora Belmont; or, The Sincere Lover. A True Story of the Heart.. 1 75
The Lover's Trials; or Days before 1776. By Mrs. Mary A. Denison, 1 75
High Life in Washington. A Life Picture. By Mrs. N. P. Lasselle, 1 75
The Beautiful Widow; or, Lodore. By Mrs. Percy B. Shelley,....... 1 75
Love and Money. By J. B. Jones, author of the "Rival Belles,"... 1 75
The Matchmaker. A Story of High Life. By Beatrice Reynolds,.. 1 75
The Brother's Secret; or, the Count De Mara. By William Godwin, 1 75
Life, Speeches and Martyrdom of Abraham Lincoln. Illustrated.... 1 75
Rome and the Papacy. A History of the Men, Manners and Temporal Government of Rome in the Nineteenth Century,.................. 1 75
Above books are each in cloth, or each one is in paper cover, at $1.50 each.

☞ **Above Books will be sent, postage paid, on Receipt of Retail Price, by T. B. Peterson & Brothers, Philadelphia, Pa.**

WORKS BY THE VERY BEST AUTHORS.

The following books are each issued in one large duodecimo volume, bound in cloth, at $1.75 each, or each one is in paper cover at $1.50 each.

The Count of Monte-Cristo. By Alexander Dumas. Illustrated,...$1 75
The Countess of Monte-Cristo. Paper cover, price $1.00; or cloth,.. 1 75
Camille; or, the Fate of a Coquette. By Alexander Dumas,......... 1 75
The Lost Love. By Mrs. Oliphant. author of "Margaret Maitland," 1 75
The Roman Traitor. By Henry William Herbert. A Roman Story, 1 75
The Bohemians of London. By Edward M. Whitty................... 1 75
The Rival Belles; or, Life in Washington. By J. B. Jones,.......... 1 75
Love and Duty. By Mrs. Hubback, author of "May and December," 1 75
Wild Sports and Adventures in Africa. By Major W. C. Harris, 1 75
Courtship and Matrimony. By Robert Morris. With a Portrait,... 1 75
The Jealous Husband. By Annette Marie Maillard,................... 1 75
The Refugee. By Herman Melville, author of "Omoo," "Typee," 1 75
The Life, Writings, and Lectures of the late "Fanny Fern,"......... 1 75
The Life and Lectures of Lola Montez, with her portrait,............. 1 75
Wild Southern Scenes. By author of "Wild Western Scenes,"...... 1 75
Currer Lyle; or, the Autobiography of an Actress. By Louise Reeder. 1 75
The Cabin and Parlor. By J. Thornton Randolph. Illustrated,..... 1 75
The Little Beauty. A Love Story. By Mrs. Grey..................... 1 75
Lizzie Glenn; or, the Trials of a Seamstress. By T. S. Arthur,..... 1 75
Lady Maud; or, the Wonder of King-wood Chase. By Pierce Egan, 1 75
Wilfred Montressor; or, High Life in New York. Illustrated........ 1 75
The Old Stone Mansion. By C. J. Peterson, author "Kate Aylesford," 1 75
Kate Aylesford. By Chas. J. Peterson, author "Old Stone Mansion,". 1 75
Lorrimer Littlegood, by author "Harry Coverdale's Courtship,"..... 1 75
The Earl's Secret. A Love Story. By Miss Pardoe,.................. 1 75
The Adopted Heir. By Miss Pardoe, author of "The Earl's Secret," 1 75
Coal, Coal Oil, and all other Minerals in the Earth. By Eli Bowen, 1 75
Secession, Coercion, and Civil War. By J. B. Jones,................... 1 75
Above books are each in cloth, or each one is in paper cover, at $1.50 each.

The Dead Secret. By Wilkie Collins, author "The Crossed Path,"... 1 50
The Crossed Path; or Basil. By Wilkie Collins,..................... 1 50
Indiana. A Love Story. By George Sand, author of "Consuelo," 1 50
Jealousy; or, Teverino. By George Sand, author of "Consuelo," etc. 1 50
Six Nights with the Washingtonians, Illustrated. By T. S. Arthur, 3 50

BOOKS FOR PRIVATE STUDY AND SCHOOLS.

The Lawrence Speaker. A Selection of Literary Gems in Poetry and Prose, designed for the use of Colleges, Schools, Seminaries, Literary Societies. By Philip Lawrence, Professor of Elocution. 600 pages..$2 00
Comstock's Elocution and Model Speaker. Intended for the use of Schools, Colleges, and for private Study, for the Promotion of Health, Cure of Stammering, and Defective Articulation. By Andrew Comstock and Philip Lawrence. With 236 Illustrations...... 2 00
The French, German, Spanish, Latin and Italian Languages Without a Master. Whereby any one of these Languages can be learned without a Teacher. By A. H. Monteith. One volume, cloth...... 2 00
Comstock's Colored Chart. Being a perfect Alphabet of the English Language, Graphic and Typic, with exercises in Pitch, Force and Gesture, and Sixty-Eight colored figures, representing the various postures and different attitudes to be used in declamation. On a large Roller. Every School should have a copy of it.......... 5 00
Liebig's Complete Works on Chemistry. By Baron Justus Liebig... 2 00

☞ Above Books will be sent, postage paid, on Receipt of Retail Price by T. B. Peterson & Brothers, Philadelphia, Pa.

WORKS BY THE VERY BEST AUTHORS.

The following books are each issued in one large duodecimo volume, bound in cloth, at $1.75 each, or each one is in paper cover, at $1.50 each.

Rose Foster. By George W. M. Reynolds, Esq.,	$1 75
The Conscript; or, the Days of Napoleon 1st. By Alex. Dumas,	1 75
Cousin Harry. By Mrs. Grey, author of " The Gambler's Wife," etc.	1 75
Saratoga. An Indian Tale of Frontier Life. A true Story of 1787,..	1 75
Married at Last. A Love Story. By Annie Thomas,	1 75
Shoulder Straps. By Henry Morford, author of " Days of Shoddy,"	1 75
Days of Shoddy. By Henry Morford, author of " Shoulder Straps,"	1 75
The Coward. By Henry Morford, author of " Shoulder Straps,"....	1 75
The Cavalier. By G. P. R. James, author of "Lord Montagu's Page,"	1 75
Lord Montagu's Page. By G. P. R. James, author of " Cavalier,"...	1 75
Mrs. Emma D. E. N. Southworth's Popular Novels. 42 vols. in all,	73 50
Mrs. Ann S. Stephens' Celebrated Novels. 22 volumes in all,	38 50
Mrs. C. A. Warfield's Works. Nine volumes in all,	15 75
Miss Eliza A. Dupuy's Works. Fourteen volumes in all,	24 50
Mrs. Caroline Lee Hentz's Novels. Twelve volumes in all,	21 00
Frederika Bremer's Novels. Six volumes in all,	10 50
T. A. Trollope's Works. Seven volumes in all,	12 25
James A. Maitland's Novels. Seven volumes in all,	12 25
Q. K. Philander Doestick's Novels. Four volumes in all,	7 00
Cook Books. The best in the world. Eleven volumes in all,	19 25
Mrs. Henry Wood's Novels. Seventeen volumes in all,	29 75
Emerson Bennett's Novels. Seven volumes in all,	12 25
Green's Works on Gambling. Four volumes in all,	7 00

Above books are each in cloth, or each one is in paper cover, at $1.50 each.

The following books are each issued in one large octavo volume, bound in cloth, at $2.00 each, or each one is done up in paper cover, at $1.50 each.

The Wandering Jew. By Eugene Sue. Full of Illustrations,	$2 00
Mysteries of Paris; and its Sequel, Gerolstein. By Eugene Sue,	2 00
Martin, the Foundling. By Eugene Sue. Full of Illustrations,	2 00
Ten Thousand a Year. By Samuel Warren. With Illustrations,	2 00
Washington and His Generals. By George Lippard	2 00
The Quaker City; or, the Monks of Monk Hall. By George Lippard,	2 00
Blanche of Brandywine. By George Lippard,	2 00
Paul Ardenheim; the Monk of Wissahickon. By George Lippard,.	2 00
The Pictorial Tower of London. By W. Harrison Ainsworth,	2 50

Above books are each in cloth, or each one is in paper cover, at $1.50 each.

The following are each issued in one large octavo volume, bound in cloth, price $2.00 each, or a cheap edition is issued in paper cover, at 75 cents each.

Charles O'Malley, the Irish Dragoon. By Charles Lever,	Cloth,	$2 00
Harry Lorrequer. With his Confessions. By Charles Lever,	Cloth,	2 00
Jack Hinton, the Guardsman. By Charles Lever,	Cloth,	2 00
Davenport Dunn. A Man of Our Day. By Charles Lever,	Cloth,	2 00
Tom Burke of Ours. By Charles Lever,	Cloth,	2 00
The Knight of Gwynne. By Charles Lever,	Cloth,	2 00
Arthur O'Leary. By Charles Lever,	Cloth,	2 00
Con Cregan. By Charles Lever,	Cloth,	2 00
Horace Templeton. By Charles Lever,	Cloth,	2 00
Kate O'Donoghue. By Charles Lever,	Cloth,	2 00
Valentine Vox, the Ventriloquist. By Harry Cockton,	Cloth,	2 00

Above are each in cloth, or each one is in paper cover, at 75 cents each.

☞ Above Books will be sent, postage paid, on receipt of Retail Price, by T. B. Peterson & Brothers, Philadelphia, Pa.

NEW AND GOOD BOOKS BY BEST AUTHORS.

Beautiful Snow, and Other Poems. *New Illustrated Edition.* By J. W. Watson. With Illustrations by E. L. Henry. One volume, green morocco cloth, gilt top, side, and back, price $2.00; or in maroon morocco cloth, full gilt edges, full gilt back, full gilt sides, etc., ...$3 00

The Outcast, and Other Poems. By J. W. Watson. One volume, green morocco cloth, gilt top, side and back, price $2.00; or in maroon morocco cloth, full gilt edges, full gilt back, full gilt sides, ... 3 00

The Young Magdalen; and Other Poems. By Francis S. Smith, editor of "The New York Weekly." With a portrait of the author. Complete in one large volume of 300 pages, bound in green morocco cloth, gilt top, side, and back, price $3.00; or in maroon morocco cloth, full gilt edges, full gilt back, full gilt sides, etc., ... 4 00

Hans Breitmann's Ballads. By Charles G. Leland. *Volume One.* Containing the *"First," "Second," and "Third Series" of the "Breitmann Ballads,"* bound in morocco cloth, gilt, beveled boards,........ 3 00

Hans Breitmann's Ballads. By Charles G. Leland. *Volume Two.* Containing the *"Fourth" and "Fifth Series" of the "Breitmann Ballads,"* bound in morocco cloth, gilt, beveled boards,.............. 2 00

Hans Breitmann's Ballads. By Charles G. Leland. Being the above two volumes complete in one. In one large volume, bound in morocco cloth, gilt side, gilt top, and full gilt back, with beveled boards. With a full and complete Glossary to the whole work,...... 4 00

Meister Karl's Sketch Book. By Charles G. Leland. (Hans Breitmann.) Complete in one volume, green morocco cloth, gilt side, gilt top, gilt back, with beveled boards, price $2.50, or in maroon morocco cloth, full gilt edges, full gilt back, full gilt sides, etc......... 3 50

Historical Sketches of Plymouth, Luzerne Co., Penna. By Hendrick B. Wright, of Wilkesbarre. With Twenty-five Photographs....... 4 00

John Jasper's Secret. A Sequel to Charles Dickens' "Mystery of Edwin Drood." With 18 Illustrations. Bound in cloth,........... 2 00

The Last Athenian. From the Swedish of Victor Rydberg. Highly recommended by Fredrika Bremer. Paper $1.50, or in cloth,....... 2 00

Across the Atlantic. Letters from France, Switzerland, Germany, Italy, and England. By C. H. Haeseler, M.D. Bound in cloth.... 2 00

The Ladies' Guide to True Politeness and Perfect Manners. By Miss Leslie. Every lady should have it. Cloth, full gilt back.... 1 75

The Ladies' Complete Guide to Needlework and Embroidery. With 113 illustrations. By Miss Lambert. Cloth, full gilt back.......... 1 75

The Ladies' Work Table Book. With 27 illustrations. Cloth, gilt,. 1 50

The Story of Elizabeth. By Miss Thackeray, paper $1.00, or cloth,.... 1 50

Dow's Short Patent Sermons. By Dow, Jr. In 4 vols., cloth, each.... 1 50

Wild Oats Sown Abroad. A Spicy Book. By T. B. Witmer, cloth,.... 1 50

Aunt Patty's Scrap Bag. By Mrs. Caroline Lee Hentz, author of "Linda," etc. Full of Illustrations, and bound in cloth.............. 1 50

Hollick's Anatomy and Physiology of the Human Figure. Illustrated by a perfect dissected plate of the Human Organization, and by other separate plates of the Human Skeleton, such as Arteries, Veins, the Heart, Lungs, Trachea, etc. Illustrated. Bound,....... 2 00

Life and Adventures of Don Quixote and his Squire Sancho Panza, complete in one large volume, paper cover, for $1.00, or in cloth,.. 1 75

The Laws and Practice of the Game of Euchre, as adopted by the Euchre Club of Washington, D. C. Bound in cloth................. 1 00

Riddell's Model Architect. With 22 large full page colored illustrations, and 44 plates of ground plans, with plans, specifications, costs of building, etc. One large quarto volume, bound,...........$15 00

MRS. SARAH A. DORSEY'S WORKS.

Each Work is complete in one large Volume.

PANOLA. *A Tale of Louisiana.* BY MRS. SARAH A. DORSEY, author of "Agnes Graham," "Athalie," "Lucia Dare," etc. Complete in one large duodecimo volume, black and gold, price $1.50.

"PANOLA" will be found to be a work of great merit, dealing with scenes and characters not often found in fiction. It is sensational, though a romance of real life. The scene and action are partly in Louisiana and partly in Paris The characters are well drawn, and the incidents, though sometimes startling, never pass the line of probability, for Mrs Dorsey, the author, is a polished scholar and a graceful writer. The following gives the heads of each chapter in the work:

TABLE OF CONTENTS.

Read the following notice of "Panola," written by Dr. Mackenzie, Literary Editor of Forney's Daily Press, who read the work in manuscript.

"PANOLA," a Tale of Louisiana, is from the pen of Mrs Sarah A. Dorsey, a talented and highly educated lady, distinguished in biography and romance. The story is very peculiar, and strikingly original, in its philosophy, its individuality of characters, and the successive steps in the narrative by which the action culminates in a very striking and most unexpected, though highly satisfactory conclusion. Life in the south-western part of Louisiana is represented with a brilliancy of description which, indeed, is word-painting of the most artistical order. Although Panola, a bright and lovely child of genius, who is a natural musician, is the principal heroine—a veritable *prima donna* in more ways than one— there is a rival, scarcely less beautiful if somewhat less excellent. There are two lovers, to maintain the balance—but the best of these has unfortunately lost the use of his limbs—like the young King of the Black Islands, of the Arabian tale, who was half man and half marble. Under such circumstances, this gentleman would scarcely have his name written, by a fashionable mother, on the list of "eligible" candidates for her fair daughter's hand! Nevertheless, he does contrive to marry the "belye of his love," to the perfect satisfaction of both, though the preliminary miracle which enabled this to be done is to be found only in the closing chapters of the story. Panola has Cherokee blood in her veins, and some of her race prove, in this story, that they indeed are "Children of the Sun with whom Revenge is virtue." The book abounds in interest—marriage, divorce, a great musician's *debut* and triumph, the alternations of various and conflicting passions— death by poison, and the already hinted punishment of the criminal.

MRS. SARAH A. DORSEY'S OTHER WORKS.

AGNES GRAHAM. *A Novel.* BY MRS. SARAH A. DORSEY. One volume, octavo, paper cover, price Sixty Cents.

ATHALIE. *"A Winter's Tale."* BY MRS. SARAH A. DORSEY. One volume, octavo, paper cover, price Sixty Cents.

LUCIA DARE. *A Novel.* BY MRS. SARAH A. DORSEY. One volume, octavo, paper cover, price Sixty Cents.

☞ *Above books are for sale by all Booksellers and News Agents, or copies will be sent to any one, to any place, postage pre-paid, on remitting the price of the ones wanted, in a letter, to the publishers,*

T. B. PETERSON & BROTHERS,

306 CHESTNUT STREET, PHILADELPHIA, PA.